Also from Indigo Sea Press
Novels by Stone Cruz

Pet the Teacher

www.indigoseapress.com

Back in the Saddle

By

Stone Cruz

Weeping Rose Books
Published by Indigo Sea Press, LLC.
Winston-Salem

Weeping Rose Books
Indigo Sea Press, LLC
931-B South Main Street, Box 145
Winston-Salem, NC 27284

First Weeping Rose Books edition published
July, 2015
Weeping Rose Books, Running Angel, and all production design are trademarks of Indigo Sea Press, used under license.

For information regarding bulk purchases of this book, digital purchase and special discounts, please contact the publisher at
www.secondwindpublishing.com

Cover design by Pan Morelli

Manufactured in the United States of America
ISBN 978-1-63066-182-3

To the lovely nurse

who understood her patient

needed healing in every

part of his being.

Chapter 1

When Lisa realized how nice the neighborhood was, she wondered why they needed her.

"These homes are really big," she muttered to herself as she eased through the subdivision looking for Trafalger Drive. "They're two or three times as big as our old house. At least. They're like mansions."

The yards were uniformly large, green and manicured. Some had terraced flowers or rock gardens. One had an arbor covered with some vine-like plant with delicate lavender blossoms.

"Oh my god, this neighborhood is gorgeous. Why would anybody here need a public health nurse?"

Around a curve that forced her to slow her old Civic to a crawl, Lisa came upon Trafalger Drive and the address she had been looking for. The wide driveway ended at a three car garage at one end of a two story structure that might have been sitting oddly on the lot, if she could have told exactly how the house was shaped. The recessed portico where she found the front door faced the driveway, but the rest of the facade seemed to be at a 90° angle to the street. Just standing and ringing the doorbell made her feel insignificant and out of place.

The evening duty nurse answered quickly. She must've been near the door, Lisa thought. She was a stout woman in her late forties who clearly had a no-nonsense attitude. Lisa wondered how much starch she had to use to keep her green scrubs so crisp and creased after working an entire night. Her name badge showed her photo, unsmiling, and her name: "Hazel Wilkes, CNA."

"You Lisa Newsome?"

"Yes. And you're—"

"Mrs. Wilkes. This way. It's like a maze getting back to your patient."

It sounded as if Wilkes was ready to be finished with her shift and gone. Was the patient that much work, or perhaps difficult to deal with?

Just like the outside of the house, the inside was not square. It was as if someone decided to build a house that defied all sense of predictability. Lisa tried to grasp the layout of the floor plan, to figure out how to get through the confusing spaces.

The older woman wordlessly led her up a broad staircase in the middle of the house. There was a landing at the top of the stairs with a series of doorways that Lisa assumed were bedrooms. Wilkes turned left on the landing and went to the last door, which stood open.

It was indeed, Lisa saw, a large bedroom, a very masculine room. Trophies adorned the dark furniture and the walls were papered with framed photos and awards. In the center of the room was a queen sized bed on which a young man slept, covered with a sheet except for his head on a pillow and his right leg, elevated on another pillow and swathed in a cast up to his knee.

Retrieving a metal medical folder from a chair just inside the door, Wilkes began to recite the patient information Lisa would need.

"Here is one Mr. Lowell Triplett Tolliver. He had orthopedic surgery yesterday to repair compound fractures of the tibia and the fibula."

"Both?" Lisa whispered.

Wilkes nodded impatiently. "After recovering from anesthesia he was released with an order for three days of home health care. He is on oral antibiotics four times daily. The patient has also been medicated through the night with hydrocodone for pain and has generally slept. As noted, I gave him 800 milligrams at 4 a.m. So chances are he'll wake up and want pain medicine within the next couple hours. Now here—" She flipped a page on the folder and pushed it into Lisa's hands. "—you'll see the doctor's orders for today. Good luck getting him awake enough to take care of these."

"What about food and drink?"

"The cupboard and refrigerator are full and we are allowed

to take whatever we want."

"No. Not us. Him. What about his intake and output?"

"Oh. Not much but water. He hasn't eaten anything. I have asked him if he was hungry in those few moments he was awake. Over twelve hours he's put out out about 1800 cc's of urine."

"So," Lisa asked, "he hasn't been much trouble?"

"None." Wilkes walked out the room toward the stairs. "See you tonight at 6:45."

"I have a couple questions," Lisa said, following the older woman as she scurried down the stairs.

"What?"

"Well is he alone in this house all by himself?"

"That depends on what you mean." Wilkes scooped up a pocketbook as she went through the enormous living room. "His parents picked him up from the hospital and brought him here. They waited until I got here a little before 7 and left. Seems they were a day late for their vacation in Santa Fe."

Lisa stopped—then immediately started walking again to catch up with her colleague. She had to call after her as Wilkes headed out the front door.

"Wait a minute. Mr. Tolliver had major surgery. His family brought him home the same day and then left on vacation?"

"That's right."

"Well if he has us for three days and nights, who's going to take of him after that?"

Wilkes, already out the door, turned back toward her with the impatient look she seemed to wear quite often. "Three days, but just two nights, young lady. I've done one of my three. In seventy-two hours you will have finished your three shifts and your work week. I suggest you don't linger on any case—and especially this one—beyond your allotted time because, frankly, there is absolutely nothing beyond that you can do about it." And having spoken her final words, she turned and walked toward her minivan in the driveway.

Lisa stood in the doorway watching as she drove away,

trying to decide if she felt more abandonment or anger. Or confusion. It made no sense whatever that a patient would live in such an opulent, elegant house and have to resort to a public health nurse. And how could any family desert a member who endured such an extensive operation just so they wouldn't miss their vacation? Perhaps it was their intention to be back by the time their son exhausted his prescribed public health nursing.

Silently she wandered through the house until she found the kitchen. She pulled open the refrigerator door to set her sack lunch inside. As Wilkes had said, it was packed with food. Name brands. Large sizes.

Lisa climbed the stairs again and went to the young man's bedroom. He was still sleeping, breathing deeply and slowly. He seemed not to have moved at all. So she picked up the file and reviewed the doctor's orders for the patient over the next seven days. If his family didn't return, who would fulfill his care, she wondered, after she was gone and he was left in this palace alone?

Lisa made a quick inventory of the supplies she would need. Beside his bed was the toilet chair she would try to get him up and onto sometime today. Beside that was the aluminum walker he was to try use tomorrow. Against the wall were the crutches he was to try to work up to eventually, though by then she would be released from his case and long gone.

She flipped the file over and began to read the portion that detailed the patient's treatment history. The surgeon had scrawled a clinical description of the injury. What caught her attention was the end of the first sentence: ". . . as a result of a kick from a horse during a rodeo competition." Was he a cowboy?

Lisa read on through the description of the surgery to the portion of the file that discussed the patient's prognosis. The text there filled her with a sense of disappointment and sadness for this young man, whom she had never spoken to or even seen awake: "Apprised patient upon his waking from procedure that the reconstruction was successful . Advised patient that he will no longer be physically able to participate in rodeo events."

She glanced toward the young man asleep in the queen sized bed. Deserted by his family and permanently handicapped by his injury. It hadn't occurred to her until that moment that those who lived in such grand homes might also suffer financial need and aloneness. On the other hand, she was acquainted with both. Being broke and alone were constant realities, at least since the divorce.

Lisa set down the file and began to walk around the bedroom, looking at the awards, trophies and framed news articles. It seemed to her the word "champion" was printed or etched or engraved on virtually everything she saw. In particular there was a magnificently gaudy belt buckle individually inscribed to her patient: "LT Tolliver, All Around Champion Cowboy." Was it actual gold and silver with diamond chips, she wondered. Surely not. If it were, he would have been able to sell it, or at least have gotten a loan against it to pay for his health insurance.

She began reading the framed articles mounted on the walls. There were multiple photos of Tolliver, in some of which he held trophies and stood alongside beautiful girls and dignified men—all dressed in western attire—and in some of which he was riding animals— large animals, horses and bulls, who did not seem pleased that he was astride them.

Lisa stopped before one news article with a photo of Tolliver in which he looked so young she thought he must have a younger brother. The headline however, confirmed his identity: "LT Tolliver Lassos National Junior Champion Crown." His patient file listed him as thirty-two, four years older than she was. As the article revealed, he had won the junior championship at sixteen. So he must've have been a rodeo cowboy for more than half his life. What could possibly take the place of it after so many years, she wondered, shaking her head.

She stood closer to the framed articles, examining his pictures closely. He was not a tall man, probably no more than 5' 9", and very lean. He seemed, even in the action photos, to be enjoying himself immensely. And in those where he was receiving awards he wore a guileless, infectious smile. LT Tolliver, she decided, was just a happy guy. She wondered if losing the ability to compete in the rodeo would steal away that joy.

Lisa had an awareness suddenly that someone was watching her. She glanced over her shoulder at the motionless cowboy. His eyes open, he stared at her. And she, surprised at his silent observance, stood staring back and saying nothing.

"Are you my new nurse?" His voice was raspy with disuse.

She turned and stepped to the side of his bed. "Hello, Mr. Tolliver. My name is Lisa Newsome. I'm your daytime public health nurse."

He looked toward the bedroom door. "So is Witch Hazel gone?"

"W—Witch Hazel? Hazel Wilkes? Yes. She left at seven."

"There is a God." He extended his arms in a sleepy stretch. "Can I have a drink of water, please?"

"Sure." She picked up the small Styrofoam pitcher sitting on the night stand beside his bed.

"No, darlin'," he said, laying his head back on his pillow and covering his eyes with one forearm. "Can I have one from my private stash. It's in an ice chest in the closet."

Her curiosity outweighing her wariness, Lisa opened his closet door. Sure enough there was a red cooler sitting in the middle of the spacious walk in. She lifted the lid to see two dozen bottles of water and sports drinks immersed in wet ice.

"Had my nephew Randy fix it up for me yesterday before the night nurse got here."

"Water?"

"Yep."

She wiped the cold liquid from the outside of a bottle with the side loose edge of her scrub blouse. "And for some reason

6

you didn't tell Mrs. Wilkes about it?" She uncapped it.

"One look at that old dog and I knew she wouldn't hunt. I had a feeling my personal water chest would have become off limits."

"I see. Let's make this a little easier for you." She set the water on the night stand and raised his shoulders with one arm, while she expertly doubled his pillow and lowered him onto it. "The way you had it hidden, I thought maybe you had beer or something like that. I can't let you have alcohol yet."

He grinned broadly. It was the happy, care free smile he wore in so many of the photos. And it was contagious. Lisa couldn't help but smile in return.

"I don't drink, ma'am."

"Lisa. Please call me Lisa. While you're awake, I need to ask you, on a scale of one-to-ten, what is—"

"Seven." He cut her off. "My pain level is seven." He took a long drink, setting the bottom of the cold bottle on his bare chest. "In my experience, the day after surgery is the most painful. And if you stay ahead of the pain for that first day, you pretty much get past it."

"So you've had surgery before?"

His big smile emerged again. He pushed the sheet down to his waist and extended his arms. White lines of surgical scars adorned him at half a dozen visible points.

"I don't know you well enough to show you the rest."

She nodded. "Well, Mr. Tolliver, you can have another pain pill now if you like. That will keep it from getting too bad."

"LT. Everybody just calls me LT."

"Okay. LT. . . . Along with the pain pill, I need to give you an antibiotic."

"Sure."

"And what else can I get for you?"

He glanced in the direction of his bathroom. "I sure need to get to the little boy's room."

"Oh. Here." She handed him the plastic urinal. "This afternoon I'll help you get up. Right now, though, you're supposed to use this."

He held the urinal by its handle, alternating his gaze from it to his nurse.

"You used it last night, didn't you? You put out 1800 cc's. Surely she didn't put you on the chair."

"No. No, I used this all right. It's just . . ."

"Oh. Would you like for me to step outside?"

"If you don't mind, miss."

"Lisa," she said, headed for the bedroom door. "I'll call you LT and you call me Lisa. Just holler."

She walked to the stairs and sat on the top step. It was only when the cold permeated her scrub pants that she realized the staircase was made of marble. Lisa shook her head. Everything in this home revealed wealth and success. Why did this cowboy need public assistance?

"Okay."

She went back to his bed, where he was holding out the urinal. Carrying it into the bathroom, she noted the amount of urine before she poured it into the toilet and flushed it.

Lisa picked up his file and made several notes, checking her watch to record the time. As she set the folder down and glanced at the bed, she realized he was watching her.

"What can I get for you, LT?"

"Would you mind giving me the remote?"

It was only then she became aware of the flat screen TV mounted on the wall. She found the remote on his dresser and handed it to him.

"Can I get you another pillow?" she asked. "Maybe I can raise your head a little?"

"In my closet," he said. "Hat rack on the right side."

When she opened the closet door again and turned on the light to look up at the shelf above his hanging clothes, she realized beyond doubt what he was. A dozen cowboy hats— straw hats, work hats with bandanas tied around them, unstained dress hats—lined the shelf. There were also a couple pillows that she quickly pulled down and took to his bedside.

Once again she wordlessly lifted his head and shoulders and placed another pillow beneath him, lining them up for the best support. It dawned on her as she was straightening the pillows that he had glanced down the loose neck of her scrub blouse. Lisa pushed the thought from her mind. Based on the position she put his head in, where else could he have looked? And, anyway, all he could have seen was her lavender sports bra.

He sighed and pushed a button on the remote. The picture came on almost instantly. It was a cable sports channel. LT dropped the remote on his chest.

"You know the trouble with this network?" he asked.

"What?"

"They never show rodeos." He yawned, a great sleepy yawn. "Thanks, Lisa. For taking good care of me."

"You're welcome. Would you like something to eat?"

". . . Later maybe."

Within two minutes he was sleeping again. She debated as to leaving the TV on or turning it off. She decided at length to leave it on, but took the remote from his chest and put it on the nightstand. As she did, he smiled in his sleep.

Once again it was the feeling she was being watched that stirred her. Sitting in the chair beside the bedroom door, listening to the drone of the television and waiting for her patient to wake and need her, Lisa had dozed. She jumped at the recognition that she had dropped off to sleep, and looked toward the bed.

Tolliver was staring at her, his hands behind his head and such a relaxed expression on his face that it seemed he must've been watching her for a while.

"Mr. Tolliver. LT." She stood and went to the bed. "Are you feeling all right?"

"Yeah."

She glanced at her watch. It was 11:30.

"It's been four hours. Are you ready for another pain pill?"

He stretched. "How 'bout if we cut one in half? I think that will do me."

She popped open the pill bottle and expertly snapped one of the tablets in half. He wagged his water bottle back and forth to demonstrate he had enough of a drink to wash down the medicine.

"You know," she said, putting the pill in his open palm, "I'm supposed to ask you your name and birthday every time I give this to you. But since you're the only person here besides me and this prescription isn't for me, I'm guessing this must be meant for you. Are you ready for something to eat yet?"

He nodded. "I could eat something."

"Do you know what you'd like?"

"How about two peanut butter and jelly sandwiches?"

"Two? Sure," she said. "Anything else to go with that?"

"Naw. I'll just start with that. Now my mom has some 'designer' jam in the fridge from some mail order house. I don't need that. There ought to be some regular grape jelly in the door. And there's white bread and smooth peanut butter in the pantry."

"Okay. May I sit up here and eat my lunch with you?"

"Oh yes, please. You can even have some of my vintage water."

Lisa smiled. "I'll be right back."

She found everything she needed in the opulent kitchen, including a wooden tray large enough to carry his plate of sandwiches and her meager lunch, which she put on a plate as well. He was patiently watching an old black-and-white movie when she came back into his room. Lisa set up a TV tray beside his bed and put his plate on it.

"Would you like another water?"

"How about one of those lemon-limes this time? And get yourself whatever you'd like."

By the time she had set a table up for herself in front of her chair against the wall, he had already wolfed down one of the sandwiches.

"Wow! Guess you haven't eaten in a while. Maybe you should have—"

"Would you hand me that." He pointed to the little plastic tray that had accompanied him home from the hospital. "Like I said, this ain't my first rodeo."

A helpless feeling came over her as she watched his body convulsed. He vomited the sandwich into the tray, gathered himself and wiped his mouth on the back of his hand.

"I'm sorry." He extended the container. "Would you flush this?"

Lisa scrambled to take away the tray. "Oh, I'm so sorry."

She dumped the remains of the sandwich in the toilet and flushed it and then rinsed out the hospital tray. By the time she walked back into the bedroom, her patient was eating his second sandwich."

"Uh. Are you sure you want to do that?"

The big smile emerged. "Pull your chair up by the bed, if you don't mind. I'm just fine."

Hurriedly, anxiously, she moved her chair and TV table   to his side, prepared for him to be sick again.

"It's okay, ma'am. Really it is. I should have warned you. The first thing I try to eat after I have general anesthetic, I always throw up. After that, I can pretty much eat whatever I want."

"Well it kind of—took me by surprise."

"Yeah. I should have said something. Terrible waste of a good sandwich."

She turned her own sandwich—a baloney and cheese she had made at 6 a.m. that morning just before rushing out the door—around and around in her hands. Finally she glanced at him and ventured a question, one of many that had come to her in the five hours since she had arrived.

"L.T., it sounds as if you have had several operations. Are those all from rodeo injuries?"

"Yes, they are pretty much." He paused, counting silently. "This was my ninth surgery—not counting that they had to fix

11

my left collar bone twice. So it's either ninth or tenth, depending on how you figure it."

"Well . . . I have a question. And I know this is none of my business. I'm just asking this because you only have nursing care for two more days after today, and no matter how well you do, you won't be well enough to take care of yourself by then at all."

He uncapped the sports bottle and casually took a long drink. "Yeah?"

"Is it because you've had so many surgeries that your family went on vacation and left you here on your own? Are they planning to be back by the time I leave for good?"

"I don't think so," he replied. "I expect they won't be back for a couple weeks at least. They always go away about this time of year."

Lisa considered his words and shook her head. "I'm sorry. I don't mean to meddle where it isn't my business, but somehow that doesn't seem right to me. When you really need them, they've deserted you."

He shrugged. "I guess there are two schools of thought on that. To you I guess it looks like my family doesn't care about me having a serious operation. On the other hand, my dad and mom never wanted me to rodeo at all. They've begged me to quit for the past dozen years and, as they see it, it's damned inconsiderate of me to get myself hurt once again right when I knew they were going away on vacation. They probably think it serves me right to need help and not have it."

"Oh," she said slowly. "Their dislike of you riding in the rodeo—is that why they haven't gotten you health insurance?"

His broad, easy smile returned and he extended his arms. "It has nothing to do with them. I'm too old to be on their policy—and anyway, if you were a health insurance company, would you sell me insurance?"

"You mean—"

"As long as I rodeo, I'm not going to get legitimate insurance. Oh sure, there are major medical policies that cover stuff. But the premiums are so high and the payout is so small for a guy like me that I'm better off not wasting my money."

"But now you'll be able to get insurance, right?"

"Now?"

She studied his face. Did he not remember what the surgeon had told him yesterday after he first woke up? Should she dare bring it up?

". . . Well, yes. Now that you . . . aren't able to ride in the rodeo anymore."

LT laughed. It was a hearty, unreserved laugh. "Oh you mean how the doctor said my riding days were over? That's the same thing they told me when the bull sat on me in Calgary and smashed my pelvis. It's the same thing they said in Tulsa when my pony threw me against the corral and broke my three favorite vertebras. And it's what they said when the bronc stepped on my shoulder in Bakersfield. They always say that shit. And I always look at it like they're trying to motivate me—you know, telling me I can't do something in order to convince me to try harder. I was thinking that was why they sent me the nurse from hell last night. Nobody would want to be sick around her."

"Does that go for me too?"

"No. You can nurse me all you want. But this whole 'three days only' thing—I look at that like they're challenging me to get better."

She considered his words. "Well, that's a hopeful attitude. Still, a compound fracture of both bones in your lower leg. It's amazing to think somebody could come back from that and still be physically able to compete in rodeo events."

He gazed at her, more serious than she had seen him. "It's not automatic, ma'am. I'm probably facing four—even six— months of hard work. But eventually I will be back in the saddle."

She stood and picked up the medical file. Flipping it open, she went down the list to remind herself of what she had to do for her patient before her shift was over.

"Well Mr.—I mean, LT, getting back into the rodeo is a worthy long-term project for you. My responsibility, unfortunately, is more immediate. My job is to help with the first steps toward getting you well. And this afternoon that means . . ." She ran her finger down the page of orders. ". . . I have to give you a bath."

First the first time, he had a stunned look of surprise. "Uh, well, just get me up into the bathroom. I can shower myself."

"Well, I'm sorry, but that's strictly prohibited for the next twenty-four hours. Really, it's not safe. The doctor's orders call for me to give you a sponge bath."

LT sighed, studying her face, trying to determine her level of resolve. "What say we skip that bath? You can just write down that you gave it to me."

"No." She shook her head. "I'm not a stickler for the rules like Mrs. Wilkes, but today a bath is a legitimate health concern for you. It says here that you have not bathed since your injury, which was four days ago." Her eyes grew wide. "Four days! You had a double compound fracture of the tibia and fibula and they let you go three days without surgery?"

"Well I was in Arizona, darlin'," he said calmly.

"Arizona?"

"Yeah. I was in a rodeo. In the bareback riding I drew a horse I have a little history with. He bucked me off backwards and, as I was sailing through the air, he kicked me like a football with his back legs."

"Well why didn't you have surgery there? Surely they have hospitals and orthopedic surgeons in Arizona."

"Oh, but I like my sawbones here. He always complains, but he does a good job of putting me all back together."

"How did you get back to Fort Worth?"

"One of my buddies brought me. I had to wait for him to finish the bull riding, but after that he drove me straight back here. And Doc operated on me right away."

"Dr. Towns? Well he's the one who ordered your bath. In fact he wants you to bathe every day. An injury and incision like yours is prone to infection. You can cut way down on that risk by keeping your body as clean as possible."

"Well." He hesitated. "I'm with you on that. Really I am. And I do need a bath. It's just . . ."

It was her turn to put her hands on her hips and give him a big smile. "You don't mean to tell me that a guy who's not afraid of rodeo bulls and wild horses is afraid of letting his nurse give him a bath."

"Hell yeah!" he exclaimed. "When she looks like you. It would be different if you were as homely as that old bag who was here last night, but you're a looker, honey."

His words gave her a strange, warm, confusing feeling. She hesitated for only the briefest moment before the nurse in her took charge again.

"Thank you for a very lovely and weird compliment. Now, however, you're going to have a sponge bath." She took a deep breath. First we have to get you onto this bath chair."

"You mean this toilet chair?"

"Doesn't 'bath chair' sound so much more appealing? Anyway it's meant for many purposes. When you get well enough to take a shower, you can take it in there with you. Helps prevent falls."

She went into his bathroom to fill the square plastic bowl that also came home with him from the hospital with warm water. As she waited for the tap water to grow warm, she found the stack of large, fluffy bath towels and took two. Lisa emerged from the bathroom to find her patient watching her with the wariness of a child waiting to be called in for a vaccination. She tried to prevent the smile that sought escape from her lips.

"I promise you, LT, this will not be painful or degrading."

He turned his head away and quietly muttered, "That ain't what I'm worried about." But he didn't say it so softly she couldn't hear.

She tried to put the comment out of her mind, just as she had dismissed his remark about her being attractive and the way he had looked down her blouse. Instead she focused on positioning the bath chair perfectly beside his bed and setting the water and soap where she could get to it easily. Lisa studied the setup, deciding if everything she needed was ready.

"So," she asked him quietly, "you have some clean underwear?"

He nodded toward his dresser. "Top right hand drawer."

She found a stack of clean white briefs and grabbed a pair. When she came to the bed, she found him eyeing her anxiously again.

"The cure for this is just to get it over with. So here's what you do: push down with your arms and slide your bottom over here with your back to me."

The cowboy did as he was told, sliding to the very edge of the bed, facing away from her. And she leaned forward, looping her arms beneath his armpits and lifting him slightly. She was surprised, lean as he was, that he was so heavy and she had to tighten her grip, forcing his back flush against her chest.

"Now as I swing you around, you can put down your good leg to steady yourself. But don't try to support yourself with it. Trust me to move you. Okay?"

"Okay."

He was, she discovered, amazingly strong and agile. He placed his hands on either side of the bath seat as she swung him onto it, perching perfectly in place. He sat motionless, clad only in his underwear and the dangling cast.

Lisa stepped away, watching him closely. "You okay there?"

"Yep. Just waiting for someone to pull the gate."

"What?"

"Oh." He chuckled. "That's a rodeo expression. It means I'm just waiting for this bull to start bucking."

"Ah. I see. Well hopefully the chair is just going to sit there and not try to throw you on the floor." She handed him one of the large bath towels. "And here's how we're going to preserve your dignity. Wrap this around your waist and you can take off

16

your shorts. Then after I wash the rest of you, you can wash your privates yourself. Okay?"

"Works for me."

He put the towel around his waist and maneuvered beneath it to slide off his briefs. An expression of pain on his face, he struggled to get them over his cast. Lisa wordlessly stooped, pulled them free and tossed them aside.

She wet the washcloth and rubbed soap on it. Lifting his arm, she cradled it in hers and began to lather it gently. Then, pressing his arm against her side so he would not lower it, she are rinsed the cloth and wiped the soap from his arm. She turned his hand palm up and cradled it in hers as she washed it.

As she stood behind him and proceeded to wash his other limbs and his chest, a change began to come over her patient. All tension fell from his body. And as he relaxed, he leaned against her. She responded by accepting the pliable weight of his lean frame. LT's facial expression into one of peace and contemplation. As Lisa observed him, she felt a calmness growing within herself as well—a sense of purpose and rightness. This was, she realized, why she had become a nurse.

Beyond that, however, was another awareness, an odd sense of connection—almost as if she and the patient somehow belonged to each other, even knew one another in a way that transcended their understood roles—patient and nurse—and all the words they had spoken to each other this day. She found this new feeling beautiful and frightening. Above all, she was sure it was strictly her experience, that the cowboy had no idea of what was going on within her.

At length she filled the cloth with soap again and began to wash his thick, short dark brown hair. He raised his chin to accommodate her and ended up leaning back until his head fell against her breasts. He straightened himself quickly, the sudden movement causing him to wince.

"Sorry," he muttered.

"It's okay."

Something else, she realized, was happening to him as she

17

rinsed the soap from his hair. He seemed to squirm and to straighten the towel around his waist. Lisa started to ask him if he were in pain and needed to lie back in the bed. Just as she was about to speak, she realized he had fluffed the towel in an effort to conceal an enormous, unmistakable erection.

Making certain not to make eye contact—or to look at him at all—she set the wash pan on the bed next to him. She rang the wash cloth as dry as she could.

"Can you reach this easily if I leave it here?"

"Yeah."

"Okay. I'll take a stroll down the hallway there. When you get finished or if you need help, just call me."

"I will."

He hadn't moved by the time Lisa left the room and walked back to her perch on three marble staircase. She sat patiently, content to wait as long as it took for him to summon her.

Much as she tried to push it from her thoughts, she couldn't forget the image of his hard penis so obvious beneath the bath towel. Such occurrences were not unheard of, or even uncommon, among patients. During her CNA training, one of her classmates came back to their small study group from a student nursing assignment with the story of a nursing home patient who had become tumescent as she had changed his clothes. The students, all young women, had tittered and joked about it, and the teacher, a middle-aged RN, just let them discuss it for several minutes. Finally she joined the conversation:

"Well, Monica, I'm glad your patient brought this up. Since most nursing students find this a hard subject to deal with, we should get right to the point."

Lisa almost laughed aloud as she remembered what the instructor had said. The older nurse was able to put the experience into perspective for them. Above all, she had said, they should not allow the erection of a patient to deter them from following through with their responsibilities.

"A patient's boner is a left-handed compliment," she had concluded. "You don't have to take it personal, because it's a natural result of you taking care of your patient. On the other hand, if you weren't taking good care of him and he wasn't enjoying it, he wouldn't get hard."

"Lisa."

LT's voice brought her back to the moment. She scrambled to her feet and hurried back to his bedroom, only to stop abruptly in the doorway. She was astonished to see him back in his bed, covered to his waist by the sheet.

"Oh. That's amazing. I guess you're okay?"

"Maybe I'm not as helpless as the doctor thinks I am."

"Okay," she replied, picking up the wash pan, clothe and towels lying on the bed. "Still, even though you are healthy and athletic, you have to be careful not to push yourself too far or take too many chances." She carried the pan into the bathroom to dump the water, speaking over her shoulder to him. "You can set yourself back by trying to do more than you're ready for."

He didn't answer her. After a minute of silence, she wondered if she had offended him and curiously looked out the barroom door toward the bed. He was staring at her with an odd expression.

"I want to thank you for the way you treated me while ago."

"What?"

He looked down. "I reckon you know what happened to me. I sort of lost control of my body. Which, by the way, was exactly why I was worried about you giving me a bath. Well the way you handled it was, was—"

"Discrete?"

"Yeah. That's a good word for it. I really am grateful to you for that."

She nodded. "It's alright. Things like that just happen. Our bodies have natural responses. They train us to expect a man's body to sometimes, you know, experience a spontaneous erection."

He gazed at her silently.

"By tomorrow," she said, her voice light, chipper, "your bath will be old hat and you won't have anything to worry about."

His face showed sudden alarm. "You're coming back, aren't you?"

"Sure."

He smiled. "I don't expect my body to be any less bothered then. Well. Tomorrow I'm getting in the tub and taking a shower."

"We'll see about that."

Chapter 2

"Is she gone?"

"Yes. Mrs. Wilkes has left the subdivision."

"Hot damn. Good news." LT propped himself up on his elbows, staring unabashed at Lisa. "Sure am glad to see you."

"Well, thank you. I'm glad to see you." She shook her head. "Can't quite figure out what's so bad about your evening nurse."

He smiled. "Well . . . maybe poor old Witch Hazel just suffers by comparison."

"How are you feeling? How is your pain on a scale—"

"Four. No worse than four. Been getting by on ibuprofen. I don't suppose you'd like to help me down the stairs?"

"Help you down the stairs? No. You can't go down the stairs. And anyway, what's down the stairs you want?"

"Real breakfast. If you'll get me to the kitchen, I'll make us some eggs, bacon, biscuits and coffee."

"I can fix that," she responded. "You just stay here. Okay?"

"Okay. There are frozen biscuits in the freezer."

"Well that does save making them from scratch. Give me twenty minutes. And behave yourself 'til I get back."

It was easier this second day for her to find what she needed in the kitchen. Still, she was surprised again by the fine quality of the cookware and the expensive foods she was preparing. The bacon was the leanest she had ever seen, seasoned with course black pepper and, according to the label, several spices she had never heard of.

As she watched over the cooking process, her thoughts floated back—as they had throughout the night—to the casual conversation and the relaxed, pleasant afternoon she had spent with LT. How odd, Lisa had thought when the evening nurse arrived, that she—unlike Mrs. Wilkes—had not wanted to leave.

All through the quiet afternoon she and her patient had

talked. He had described his passion for rodeo, how it had grown as he had matured from an adolescent to a young man. And as his dedication to the sport swelled, the disapproval expressed by his parents grew as well.

She recognized that he was oddly humble. As he spoke about the rodeo, he never mentioned his accomplishments. He only spoke of them euphemistically, saying that he had "done all right in the nationals," or that he had been "lucky enough to win the overall championship." Finally she pointed out that the walls of his bedroom belied his humility, that they were covered with awards and glowing accounts of his many exploits.

He actually blushed. His voice was sheepish as he said, "My sisters put those old ones up. They're kind of proud of me. And my nephews and my niece have kept putting up the new stories. They think I'm the family hero. My folks think I'm the black sheep."

Lisa had given her head a shake. "Just shows how out of touch I am. I don't know the first thing about rodeo. And here I am nursing a celebrity."

"About that," he replied. "We been doing all this talking about me. I'm curious about you. And I bet you're a lot more interesting than I am."

She shook her head vigorously. "Not hardly."

"Did you always want to be a nurse?"

"Well I'm not a nurse, not yet anyway. I'm a certified nursing assistant, a CNA. During the school year, I work at night and take classes during the day to become an RN. I have one more year. Then I'll be a real nurse. But during the summer when school is out, I make my tuition money by working as a public health nurse."

He had a look of genuine admiration. "So you always wanted to be a nurse?"

The slightest dark wave swept over her face. "I do now."

"Now? What did you used to want?"

". . . I used to be a stay-at-home mom with my two little

girls. Then . . . I got a divorce. I had to support myself."

LT had stared at her, clearly struggling with how to respond. "Well. Motherhood's loss is nursing's gain."

Lisa had chuckled. "Thanks."

It had given her a warm, affectionate feeling, a feeling that stole back to her chest as she finished preparing their breakfast and placed everything on one of the ornate wooden bed trays. She carried it up the stairs into his bedroom and, as she came through the door, he turned off the TV and dropped the remote on the bed.

"Smells good and looks good," he said.

"I found a couple tomatoes that weren't going to last much longer." Lisa set the little wooden platform across his thighs. "So I sliced them too. Don't know if you like 'em."

"They smell vine ripe. Nothing's better." He scooted up straight in the bed. "Pull up your chair and tray, will you?"

"Apart from having to tolerate Mrs. Wilkes, did you have a good night?"

"Pretty good. Boy, you did good with these eggs."

"How can you mess up scrambled eggs?"

He laughed. "My mom knows. She's perfected kitchen disasters."

"Well then who does the cooking? Somebody who knows her way around the kitchen has set it up and outfitted it with everything."

He nodded. "That would be 'Lupe the Great', our housekeeper. She's the little sister of Constanza."

"Who?"

"Constanza. She and her husband Felipe are—dear friends of mine. I'll have to introduce you."

She was staring at him. When he looked at her, she dropped her eyes to her plate. The irony of his words struck him then.

"Oh, that's right. Three days. . . . Check that. Two days."

"Why isn't Lupe here now? She could help care for you after my time is over."

"Ha. She always takes her vacation when my folks go

away. And anyway, my folks tell her they will fire her if I'm laid up and she helps me in any way."

"Oh my god," she said slowly. "Why would they say that?"

He took a bite of the sliced tomatoes. "They believe that I'm completely irresponsible. They think, if I'm going to get busted up like this, then it's up to me to take care of myself."

"Well, and I'm not trying to be critical of your folks, but who is going to watch out for you when I'm gone."

The boyish, beautiful smile broke across his face. "Oh, I reckon I'll get by. Always do." He gazed at her. "It's so kind of you to worry about me."

The delightful feeling of affection spread through her chest again, this time stronger and sweeter. She drew a quick breath to push it away.

"Well," she said, "what's the point of giving you the best nursing care if you're going to die of neglect afterwards?"

Once again he smiled broadly. "Reckon I'm just going to have to come stay with you. Ha. That'd give those little girls something to talk about. How old are they?"

"They are seven and five." She stooped and picked up her purse, slipping a wallet sized picture from the billfold. Holding it out to him, she said, "Nita is the older one. Nellie is the toe head."

"A spitting image of her mom." He held the photo, examining it closely. "Beautiful girls you got there, Lisa."

"Thanks."

"So Nita is actually Anita?"

"Right."

"What's Nellie short for?"

"Just Nellie. I had a great aunt named Nell. I loved her so."

"Do they like horses?"

"Of course. They're girls. Not that they've been riding all that often. Just at the state fair, you know."

"I got horses they can ride." He yawned, a big, unabashed yawn. "Maybe sometime you can bring 'em riding."

She nodded. "Perhaps so. Would you like your remote?"

24

Weariness seemed to have descended upon him suddenly. He contemplated her question for several seconds.

"Yeah. If you don't mind."

She turned on the sports network and handed him the remote. "I don't mind at all."

Within five minutes he was snoring gently. She smiled and sat in her chair by the door, her arms crossed.

He slept until just after noon and woke hungry. She offered him BLT sandwiches, to which he instantly agreed. An odd feeling of contentment settled over her as she stood before the gas stovetop preparing their lunch. And bittersweet beneath the serenity was the awareness she would only have one more day to care for him. Only one more day to enjoy his spontaneous, carefree personality.

Whatever she had been feeling in the kitchen, she was startled to climb the stairs with their meal and find LT, wearing only his skivvies, moving around his bedroom on crutches. She gasped.

"Oh," he said, "looking over his shoulder at her. "You want me to put on some britches?"

"It's not that," she replied. "I mean, I've never seen you when you were wearing anything but your underwear. I was just surprised to see you up on your crutches."

He swung around in a wide circle. "It's like riding a bull. After you do it once, you never forget how."

"So you've been on crutches before?"

"Couple times. Three or four maybe."

"Okay, LT. Well that's not a weight bearing cast. So you have to keep from stepping down with your right foot." She set the food tray on the bed. "Want some lunch?"

He swung himself to the bed, fell into it backwards and immediately sat up straight. Scooping the first of his two sandwiches, he began to eat it rapidly, vigorously. His nap, Lisa could see, had restored his energy.

"I've fixed bacon for you twice in one day," she said.

"Hope you don't OD."

LT laughed. "Death by bacon. What a cowboy way to go." He swallowed a bite and followed it with a big drink of water. "Far as I can tell, this sandwich is paradise on toast."

"I'm glad you like it."

"I'm glad you take such good care of me."

"Well . . . it's my job. And it's what I like to do. And you're . . . you know, easy to take care of."

"Really? 'Cause some nurses, like old Witch Hazel for instance, have given me the idea that I might be sort of a pain in the ass."

She smiled. "Not with me, you haven't been a pain. You've been cooperative and pleasant."

He looked at her skeptically. "Even when I was fighting with you about you giving me a bath?"

Lisa sighed. "About that. As soon as you finish your lunch—right now, from the look of it—I have to give you another sponge bath."

"Naw, not today. I mean, I enjoyed you giving me a bath yesterday. Obviously. But today I'm mobile. I can move around real well. And I'm steady on my feet—or crutches. Like I just showed you."

"Nice try, Mr. LT, but you know you can't take crutches into the shower with you."

"I have a large shower stall."

She shook her head, wearing the expression she acquired when one of her daughters tried to convince her of something absurd. "Those crutches are not designed for slick, wet surfaces. Try to use them in there and you'll fall flat on your ass. And that cast may be water proof, but you can't stand up on it to support yourself."

He shrugged. "So I'll put the shower chair in there and sit on it."

"You mean I could put it in the shower for you, don't you? The danger is getting into and out of the shower, not to mention turning the water on and off and adjusting it. I came here to

26

help you get well, not to let you fall into another injury."

"What difference does it make? After tomorrow you'll be gone. How am I going to take a shower then?"

She felt the same pang of regret that had come over her while she was preparing their meal. "I—I don't have any control or responsibility for that. For right now, though, you're my patient. And I'm taking care of you the best way I can."

His face softened momentarily. "You've taken very good care of me, *Azulita*."

"What? What did you call me?"

"Oh. Sorry. Uh. I have this bad habit of nicknaming people sometimes."

"What did you call me?"

"It wasn't bad or nothing. I called you *Azulita*, which sort of means 'little blue eyes' in Spanish."

". . . Oh. Oh, that's sweet. That's . . . sweet of you. Still, though, I'm not letting you get in the shower by yourself."

He gazed at her and the boyish smile emerged. "Then you get in there with me."

She recoiled. "Oh really now. You can't be serious."

"Serious as a broken leg. You can turn the water on and off and get me situated in the shower chair. That way I could take my shower and you wouldn't have to worry about me falling."

"That's the silliest thing I've ever heard." She tugged on the bottom of her blouse. "These scrubs are all I've got to wear. I don't have a change of clothes. And, getting into a shower with a patient, I can't even imagine how unprofessional— maybe even unethical—that would be."

He leaned forward. "Look, you don't have to get your clothes wet at all. You saw how big those bath towels are, right? Well in the top drawer of that dresser are some big safety pins. I use them to pin my jeans when I can't get a pants leg over a cast. You could use those pins to fasten one of those towels around you tight as you want." He threw his hands up, as if to proclaim his sincerity. "And I won't try nothing. I won't touch nothing. I won't even look at nothing."

27

They stared silently at each other. When LT realized she was actually considering the possibility, he spoke up again.

"You could teach me the safe way to get in and out of the shower for when you aren't here to help me."

Lisa sighed. "You know there are rules against this."

"Who am I going to tell? You're the one who's a stickler for the rules."

". . . And you realize, if this ever got back to my agency, I'd say you made the whole up? This job is my livelihood and I can't afford to lose it—or my reputation."

"Got it."

Wordlessly she went to the dresser and found the safety pins he had described. She didn't look at him as she went into his bathroom and closed the door.

As she pulled off her scrubs she thought about leaving on her bra and panties. They would surely get wet, though. And how uncomfortable they would be for the remaining six hours of her shift. So she stripped completely and stood naked as she folded her clothes and put them in a drawer. Somehow keeping them neat and hidden away made what she was about to do seem slightly less questionable. She pulled a fluffy towel from the stack and wrapped it as tightly around herself as she could and still be able to move her arms and legs. Pinning the flap along her right side—though it made her breasts more prominent—also made any revealing gaps less likely. She made a mental note not to turn her back to the cowboy, and especially not to turn her back and bend over.

Lisa made it a point, as she opened the bathroom door and walked over to the bed to pick up the shower chair, to appear as businesslike as possible. From the corner of her eye, she could see that the cowboy, good to his word, was standing on his crutches by the dresser, holding a clean pair of underwear and not staring at her. Neither spoke, intent on preserving the dignity and decorum they had agreed upon.

She placed the chair in the stall just behind the drain, where she could adjust the spray onto him and made sure it sat level on the tile floor of the stall. After being certain there were soap, shampoo and a wash cloth, she turned on the water. As she stood, her hand under the flow, she heard the sound of his crutches on the bathroom floor.

"All right." Her voice was subdued. "I think the water's about right. Can you take off your—" She had glanced toward him and saw that he was completely naked, his clean underwear in one hand. "Oh. So you got 'em off by yourself. That's good. You're making progress." She silently congratulated herself on not showing any emotional response to the incredibly erotic sight of his penis hanging before her.

She stepped behind him, taking his clean briefs and putting them on the bathroom countertop as if this situation—wrapped only in a towel alongside a nude, amazingly attractive patient— was the most normal thing in a nurse's day. Taking his crutches and setting them against the wall, she lifted his right arm and put it around her shoulder.

"I'm just going to guide you and show you the safe way in and out of the shower. So lean on me and make sure to keep your right foot elevated. You're going you have the urge to go down—to stand on it. And that's the biggest mistake you can make right now."

"Well, maybe not the biggest," he muttered.

He situated most of his weight on his good leg and reached up with his free arm to grip the top of the aluminum frame of the stall. His right arm, draped around her right shoulder was intentionally held at angle, she realized, so his hand did not come near her breast. Once again she was surprised by his strength and the ease with which he maintained his light pressure against her side. His touch was thrilling to her, even as purposefully innocent as it was. And she was committed to keeping the awareness of her excitement to herself.

"You can put your hand on the far arm of the chair for balance. . . . That's good. Try not to lean you weight on it. Just steady yourself. . . . And sit down. . . . Good."

Once he was safely perched on the seat, Lisa maneuvered

the shower head so he would be in the stream without the water hitting him right in face.

"Is that okay?" she asked. "It's not too hot?"

"It's just fine ma'am."

Standing by his side where he could not see her face, she smiled. "Okay. If you'll sit still, I'll do the work."

As she squeezed shampoo into her hand, she became aware that the towel around her had already become saturated. And already it had grown heavy and loose. It would be difficult to move around him without the towel sagging. If it drooped, she would be forced to hold it in place with her elbows while she bathed him. The best bet was to work as quickly as possible.

He leaned his head back as she lathered his hair. A great sigh moved through his body. She pushed his head forward, his face down, into the stream of warm water to rinse the soap from his hair. Then she ran water through the wash cloth to soap his upper body.

"Twice."

"What?"

"My hair tends to be oily. I have to shampoo it twice."

"Oh. Sure. I can do that."

At the precise moment he leaned his head back—as he had the first time—and she raised her arms to rub in the shampoo, the towel sagged in front of her breasts. To keep from being exposed, she quickly leaned her chest against the back of his shoulders. She raised the towel swiftly with one hand, playing out off as of the touch had been unintentional. Still, the boy straightened for an instant. He exhaled, seemingly deep in thought.

After she lathered and rinsed his hair again, she worked soap into the washcloth and ran it across his shoulders, back and chest. Despite herself, as she was running clean water on his abdomen to get all the lather off, she glanced quickly down at his crotch. When she saw no evidence of tumescence, she didn't know whether to feel relief or disappointment.

Lisa lifted his arm and he held it out, extended from his

body, as she soaped it and rinsed it. She unfolded his hand, washing the back and palm of it and between his fingers. For some reason she found holding his hand strangely sensual, so she made sure not to make eye contact. After washing the other arm and hand, she stepped to one side before him, in order not to block the flow of warm water onto him, and knelt to wash his legs and feet.

She washed his left thigh and knee and his good calf and foot, and she stood quickly. When she did, the heavy towel slid down. Lisa caught her breath and froze, realizing that one of her breasts had become completely exposed. It was only a few inches from his cheek, a glistening, dangling orb specked and splattered with water, and crowned with a hot pink areola. She remained motionless. Nothing in her training had prepared her for a moment like this. And she hoped against hope the cowboy didn't realize the protruding nipple was a giveaway of her state of sexual arousal.

Wordlessly LT reached over, grasping the towel beneath her armpit and lifting it gently so that her breast was once again concealed. This time she could not help but make eye contact with him.

He shrugged. "So okay. We're even, *Azulita*."

". . . Thanks."

She crossed to his side and knelt again. Soaping the washcloth, she began to clean his right leg from the hip down.

"I know it's a waterproof cast," she said, "but I don't want to get any more moisture in it than necessary. It becomes really itchy and uncomfortable, not to mention that it can start to smell a little like a wet dog. I can tell you how to deal with that, though." She washed between the toes that protruded from the fiberglass. "Are your little piggies ticklish, LT?"

It dawned on her that he wasn't responding and she started to look up to his face when suddenly she found herself staring at his erect penis. Once again she became immobile. What she do, she asked herself. Should she ignore the curved, wickedly stiff member inches from her face? Should she excuse herself

31

from the shower, go into another room until it dispersed of its own accord, or he took care of it? She played out the possibilities. If she left the bathroom, she was going to have to get back into the shower eventually to get him out. She cringed at the notion of walking through the house draped in a wet towel, dripping water as she went. It was probably out of the question for him to masturbate with her in his presence.

Full of questions and uncertainty, Lisa looked up to see him looking down at her. He smiled sheepishly.

"I guess there's no denying how attractive I find you. I told myself I could control it so this wouldn't happen," he said.

As if to distract them both from the fierce condition he was experiencing, he continued. "Me and the boys were waiting out the time before the finals—I think it was in Casper. Anyway, there we were, just a couple dozen cowboys watching TV. And this commercial came on for one of those boner pills, you know. The announcer says, 'Seek medical attention for a hard on lasting more than four hours.' One of my buddies says, 'Man, if I get a four hour woody, I'm not calling the doctor, I'm calling the newspaper.'"

They both laughed, and he went on, "But then Stew, one of the guys, says, 'Not me. If I get a four hour hard on, I'm going straight to the emergency room and find the prettiest nurse there and say, ma'am, can you help me with this?'"

". . . Well," Lisaspoke slowly, her words measured, "' . . . I'm the only nurse here, but I'm pretty sure I can help you with this condition."

They gazed at each other.

"Oh course, once I leave tonight, none of this—I mean none of it—ever happened."

He nodded. "I understand. . . . You can trust me."

She put abundant soap on her hand and built warm lather and gently clasp his cock. He moaned and leaned his head back. His penis had appeared hard and full, but at her touch it swelled, bent and stiffened all the more. He opened his legs and she leaned against his thigh.

Gently at first, she began to stroke him, caressing the length of him with supple, pliant fingers. She lifted his scrotum with one hand, gently massaging his testicles, sliding the other the all the way down the erect member. The motion caused the towel to fall, exposing not one but both breasts, but this time she did nothing to conceal herself. Their appearance, she thought, might hasten his climax.

Only it didn't. The cock seemed only to grow harder in her hand. She looked up from her manipulation to see his eyes move from her breasts to her eyes. His face was filled with longing.

Lisa looked back to the thick, engorged organ in her grasp. How long could he hold out, prolong this moment that was both awkward and enticing? She must, she realized, increase the stimulation.

She let go of him abruptly—which caused him to jump. Cupping her hands, she gathered water from the stream and splashed it on his privates—which made him jump again—to cleanse them of soap. Then she leaned forward and slid his dick into her mouth. A jolt like an electric shock ran through him, followed by a sound that was somewhere between a cry of despair and a moan of complete ecstacy. His lower back arched as he gently eased his cock forward as far as it would go into her mouth.

Lisa sucked tightly on the head of his penis, then slackened the suction and ran her tongue along the bottom of it, pressing up on the thick vein that ran the length of the shaft. She grasped it in her fingers again, straightening so she could inspect it. Sure enough, as she slid her fingers from the scrotum to the glans, a thick, lazy drop of fluid appeared at the tip. As she leaned forward and ran the cock deep into her mouth, she asked herself if she should let him ejaculate in her mouth or not. It was, she decided long past the time of preserving decorum or professional distance. Did it really matter now if she swallowed his cum? And maybe still kept sucking him, just to drive him mad?

She situated herself fully between his legs, pressing herself against him, making sure her breasts rubbed against the sensitive skin on the inside of his thighs. And, as she felt the slight rocking motion of his hips, moving his member back and forth in her mouth, she waited for the hot burst of his orgasm. Only he did not cum. In fact he stopped moving altogether.

Leaning back, the back of her head fully in the warm stream of the shower, she looked up at him in alarm. Had her wanton display shocked him, disgusted him? Had she so crossed a line that he found her repulsive?

He put his hands under her elbows. "It can't be comfortable like that on your knees," he said, lifting her to her feet.

As she stood, the towel fell all the way to her ankles. He stared at her naked before him. His expression was unconcealed delight. And desire.

"You're going to trip over that towel, *Azulita*. And you know, it's safety first around here." He pulled his knees together. "Now put your right foot there by my good leg. And put your other foot over here, but be careful you don't scrape yourself on that rough old cast."

The slightest hint of a smile flashed across her face add she stood before him. "That's a sweet idea, rodeo boy. Very appealing, but the arms on that chair won't let me sit on your lap like that."

LT stared at her. His face was full of awe and joy. And desire. Putting his hands on the aluminum arms of the chair, he pushed to his feet—something that made Lisa catch her breath and look down to make sure his cast wasn't on the tile floor.

He draped a hand on the top of the shower door again and with his free hand he grasped her hand and drew her to him, their faces inches apart. She felt his hand slide up her arm, to her shoulders and behind her neck. Then her closed his eyes and kissed her—a long, firm, fulfilling, very wet kiss.

"Words ain't my strong suit," he said softly, "so it doesn't quite capture my meaning when I say, you have no idea just how beautiful you are."

An image of how she must look—hair wet and flattened against her head, no makeup, completely naked with a towel strewn around her ankles—flashed through her mind, and she replied quietly, "Maybe we should forget about your leg and have your eyes checked out."

LT smiled. "My eyes are just fine. And everything about you . . . is just so very fine, *Azulita*."

He took a breath and leaned forward and kissed her breast. It was less a kiss than a feast. His lips ran around the roundness of it, and then his tongue along the same path, and up from the bottom to the areola, moving more slowly as he progressed, until he lifted the erect nipple with the bend of his tongue. Then he situated his mouth on the nipple, sucking in gently as his tongue caressed the tiny bumps that emerged. Lisa felt her own eyes close and something like a whimper came from her throat. She leaned against him, her other breast brushing his lean chest and the hard, crooked penis pressed along her mons.

"Let's go to the bed," he whispered.

Her breath was a stutter. "Hold on and I'll get your crutches and dry towels."

"Fuck the towels and crutches." He slid the door open. "Just let me lean on you."

"We're so wet."

"Not like we're gonna be."

It was a strange procession, Lisa thought: the cowboy leaning on her as she took small careful steps, his engorged cock flopping side-to-side with each movement, all the while copiously dripping water as they made their way to his bed. And when they came to the foot of it, he let go of her while somehow turning her swiftly, effortlessly. She fell onto the rumpled sheets on her back, completely startled. One hand on the bed to support himself, he looked down at her, his expression one of thirst and—it almost seemed to her—love.

"Ever hear that expression, *Azulita*, 'sauce for the goose is sauce for the gander'?"

"Yes."

He nodded. "Well it's the gander's turn to taste the sauce."

LT slid onto to the bed between her feet, gradually moving toward her body, his eyes upon hers, spreading her legs as he moved up. As she watched him, an incredible thrill of anticipation fluttered in her chest. She realized she was holding her breath, her nipples hard, round stones. And as she watched, his mouth descended upon her vagina. He bit playfully on the hair covered mound of Venus, then slid his tongue along the slick edges of her lower lips, cupping beneath her clit and pressing upward against it. An uncontrollable relaxation washed through her limbs and body. She seemed to sink deeper into the bed.

Lisa felt his tongue search within her passage. In response, though through no conscious will, she felt her hips rise at his embrace, opening, welcoming. She watched as he sucked her clitoris between his lips and slowly slipped his middle finger upside down into her vagina. She felt it curve along the upper wall of the passage and the sweet upward pressure together with the back and forth motion as he caressed her clit with his tongue. She closed her eyes, raising her chin and giving a long sighing moan. He was content to continue stroking and kissing her sex for long minutes as she lay compliant before him, receiving his embraces as if a long felt thirst was being quenched. And, at the same time she realized the flow from within her had grown thicker and more potent, she also realized she was going to do what he had not done. She was going to cum in his mouth.

Lisa began helpless, almost panicked movements. Surely he didn't realize her orgasm was coming, did he? She should break away from him, shouldn't she? Yet her wiggling and pushing against him, against the inevitability of her climax, only caused him to force his finger firmer against the secret place deep within her and flatten his tongue against the flooding gates of her pussy. And suddenly she stopped resisting the quake he was creating within her and, to her own amazement, she put her hands on the back of his head and held his face tightly against her genitals. The climax racked her limbs, rolling through her in successive, ecstatic waves that sapped the strength from her limbs, leaving her spread and motionless.

For a minute she lay with her eyes closed. The only sound and movement was the thrilled breathing coming from her rising and settling chest. She felt tears, beautiful joyous tears, run from the edges of her eyes. And when she looked up at him at last, he was propped on his hands, gazing down at her. The boyish smiled emerged.

"My turn?"

She stared at him, almost as if she was seeing him for the first time. A new powerful emotion surged within her. She wanted him as she had never wanted anyone or anything else. She wanted to take him, all of him, inside her and hold the hot sweetness of him there.

Lisa lifted her arms to him. "Make love to me, rodeo boy. Cum in me. Fill me."

He crawled upward over her slowly until his face was directly above hers. With one hand, he lifted her leg, sliding it over his hip.

"Wrap your legs around my waist," he said softly. "I don't want my cast to scuff you up."

Awash in tranquility, she wrapped her legs around his lean waist. They stared at each other. Slowly, silently, he leaned forward and kissed her. She tasted a randy, salty marinade on his lips and tongue. It was, she knew, the effluence of her pussy, her climax. And instantly she was aroused again, seized again with the desire to be filled with him.

She felt his lower back dip slightly, then the round touch of his glans on the saturated lips of her vagina. He eased forward then, the whole, surprisingly long, hard length of his dick sliding into her. Lisa heard herself moan. As, spontaneously, her legs embraced him, her inner lips gripped the shaft within her. She pulled him down onto her, kissing him wantonly, pressing their bodies tightly together and pulling her hips upward against him again and again rapidly.

"Oh. . . . *Azulita*." His breath came in shallow draws. "I'm afraid you kind of got me worked up here, girl. I'm afraid . . . Oh-oh."

The walls of her passage seemed to have tightened firmly on him, so she could feel his cock thrusting deep within her, the pounding coming swifter and swifter until it was frantic. And then she came again, crying out, her labia seizing the phallus powerfully. At that moment the cowboy came as well, locking his hands beneath her buttocks and holding her immobile against him. Shivering then, he began to move in and out of her again as her limbs grew flaccid, sagging away from him.

Above her, he shivered and became motionless, as if recovering from a blow, and moaned. "Oh . . . Lisa. . . . Oh my god, sweet little *Azulita*."

He resumed his rocking motion, the thick penis embracing and thrilling the sated flesh, their genitals awash in their mingled liqueurs. Strength slowly came back into her limbs and she closed her legs and arms around him again.

His eyes closed, he breathed deeply, calming himself. He rolled onto his right side, straightening himself and holding her, his penis still within her, tightly to him. With his left hand, he pulled the sheets over them.

"Is it alright if we just lay here together like this for a while?"

"It's fine with me."

She lay watching him as relief, fatigue and peace washed over his face. Within two minutes he was asleep. The exquisite feeling of her orgasms and the boy's affections wearied Lisa as well. She rested her head on the pillow and in a moment she too slept.

Chapter 3

On Thursday morning, by the time she reached the subdivision where LT lived, Lisa had managed to stop sobbing.

Still, she realized as she looked at her face in her rear view mirror, it would be obvious to any observant person that she had been crying. She took a number of deep breaths and wiped her eyes again with her last crumpled tissue. At least she wasn't wearing any makeup that would run and smear.

She shook her head as she gripped the steering wheel. It had been her intention to wear at least a little makeup on this last morning, this last day of caring for the delicious cowboy. Even though she wasn't supposed to, she had intended to bring perfume and dab on a hint of it after the night nurse left and before she went up to his bedroom, the beautiful place where they shared themselves with one another repeatedly until it was almost time for Nurse Wilkes to arrive. Yes, she had hoped they might make love again this day and sweetly culminate their final day together.

That was what she had been thinking of all the way to her little rent house Wednesday evening. Then she got home and saw the letter from Keith. She was calling him on her cell phone before she finished reading it. He answered immediately, as if he had been anticipating her call—as if he had been looking forward to her outrage.

"Why am I not surprised that you called?" were his first words.

And Lisa could feel the tears pooling even before she spoke. "Keith, you know I'm supposed to have the girls this weekend." Her voice cracked despite her effort to maintain her calm. "This is three times in a row. I had lots of things planned for them."

She knew exactly the uncaring expression he was wearing even though she could not see him as he spoke. "It's not convenient."

Lisa had to gather herself, to stop crying. "My girls need their mother."

"Oh, I don't know. They seem to be thriving without you."

"I need them." A note of pleading was clear in her voice.

He snorted. "Maybe if you'd thought about the consequences, you'd have been a better wife."

Suddenly she was more angry than hurt. "You know this violates the judge's order."

Keith's tone was completely casual. "Sue me then. You'd better remember, though, how much it costs to hire a lawyer. And also, ex-wifey, you'd best remember that things don't work out so well for you in the courtroom."

More words had passed between them, things she scarcely remembered because she had been so upset. And, driving to LT's house Thursday morning, recalling bits of the conversation threw her into despair again. Lisa clenched her jaw, determined not to reveal her emotional state.

Whether it was because she was simply glad that her twelve hour shift was over or because she was oblivious to the feelings of others, Nurse Wilkes said nothing about Lisa's puffy face and red eyes. She handed over the clipboard with the previous evening's notations and walked out the front door to her car.

Lisa went into the spacious kitchen and put her sack lunch in the refrigerator. She sighed. It was time to check on her patient.

She walked through the dining room into the atrium and stopped. LT, crutches lying beside him, was sitting on the bottom step of the stairs, dressed in a T-shirt, blue jeans and with a worn, suede cowboy boot on the foot that was not swathed in a cast.

"How did you get down those stairs?" The emotions of the moment and the tenderness of the prior afternoon were pushed aside. Her tone was strictly that of an authoritative, concerned nurse.

"On my butt," he replied casually. "One step at a time. Even I ain't dumb enough to climb down these marble stairs on crutches."

". . . Oh."

He cocked his head to one side. "You been crying. . . . I hope it's not because of me."

She shook her head. "No. Well, yes. It's partly because of you."

"Because you think you violated your professional vows by making love with me? Because you think it's going to come back on you?"

"No." Her voice was definitive. "Maybe I should be worried about that, but I'm not."

"What then?"

Lisa averted her eyes, feeling inside the pockets of her scrubs for a spare tissue. "Part of why I'm upset is because this is my last day to be your nurse. I'm going to miss you. I don't think I'll ever have another afternoon like we had yesterday. It was wonderful for me."

He nodded solemnly. "Me too. But that's not all?"

"No." She began to cry again. "My ex. He isn't going to let me have my girls this weekend."

"Oh." LT frowned. "So how often does he have them?"

"Keith has custody of them."

". . . Oh."

"The judge said I'm supposed to have them two weekends every month. But Keith won't give them to me. I haven't seen them at all the last three times I was supposed to have them."

". . . Well if you don't mind my asking, why is he refusing to give them to you?"

She drew a deep breath. "He says it isn't convenient."

He gazed at her, trying to understand. "You mean he's just defying the judge because he doesn't feel like giving you your daughters for the weekend."

She nodded.

"Well," he smiled, "what does the judge think of that?"

She shook her head. "He just dares me to try to take him to court. He knows I don't have the money for a lawyer."

LT studied her silently. At length he pulled himself to his

41

feet, picked up his crutches and positioned them under his arms.

"Not to change the subject, but I been thinking about this being our last day too. I was thinking we might take a little road trip."

"Road trip?"

"Yeah. You can drive a truck, can't you?"

"Well, yeah."

"Good. 'Cause I have my right foot in a cast and I'm really not supposed to drive."

Lisa was trying to decide if what he was asking was something she could oblige. "Where is it you want to go? How long will it take?"

"All day. I was thinking that would be okay. I mean, since technically you are supposed to nurse me until 7 this evening."

She nodded. "I'm supposed to be your nurse. 'Nursing' you means something different. You are mine until 7. Where do you want to go?"

His face brightened. "I thought I'd introduce you to those friends of mine I told you about."

"You mean Constance—"

"Constanza. And her husband Felipe. The Garzas."

"And where do they live?"

"Oh just out of town, twenty-five miles or so. They live on my ranch and take care of it."

". . . You have a ranch?"

"And my pony Rex. You need to meet him too." He started toward the kitchen. "This is the way to the garage. We really should get started."

"Well wait," she said quickly. "I don't mind taking you to see your friends. And your horse, I guess. But I'm just wearing scrubs. I can't, you know, meet a lot of people."

"Okay," he replied undeterred. "So why don't we go by your place first. You can change."

"Uh . . . my place is a mess. I wasn't expecting—"

"It's okay. I'll wait in the truck."

She sighed. "All right, then."

His full size white pickup was parked in the fourth slot of the garage, farthest from the kitchen door. They walked past two SUVs and a sports car of a sort she had never seen on the way to his dusty truck.

"That's my littlest sister's Porsche you were looking at."

"It looks expensive."

"Yep. I could've bought a condo for what Pop paid for that."

The slowly rising garage door brought Lisa's old Honda into their sight. She was a little embarrassed by it, after ogling the waxed, red performance car.

LT pulled open the passenger door of his truck and lifted himself in, tossing his crutches into the bed. "I know from experience they won't fly out. So just take us to your place first."

She had to slide the bench seat forward before backing out of the garage, then heading slowly out of the subdivision. For his part, LT seemed happily at ease, scooting toward her and propping up his broken leg on the bench seat.

"So," he said, "recognizing this is none of my business— and you can tell me to back off—I'm curious as to how your ex managed to end up with custody of your children."

She shook her head, gazing down the street before her. "Keith can be a very charming, convincing guy. I knew him since we were teenagers. He was always the heartthrob when we were in high school. I should have paid attention to the fact that all the girls he dated hated him after they broke up. Instead, when he asked me out and then wanted to get serious, wanted me to marry him, I thought I was the luckiest girl in the world.

"And when he started berating me—you know, telling me I was unattractive, that I was stupid, that I was a bad wife and mother—I believed all that. When I caught him cheating, he told me he wouldn't have if I had been better in bed, if I were more attractive. I believed that too. He was fucking around and I believed out was all my fault.

"Eventually though, the lights turned on for me." She

43

glanced at the cowboy, who was listening to her silently. "It was when he took up with Shelli, a gorgeous girl in his office, and I learned he was saying all the things to her he once said to me. I took the girls and moved out.

"That had a strange impact on him. Later I realized it was because someone was actually saying 'no' to him. Keith is the one who makes all those decisions, you see. He's the one who says 'no.' Nobody says 'no' to him. Nobody walks out on him." She sighed. "I figured that out too late. He promised me he would change. Said I should give him a second chance for the sake of the girls."

Lisa gripped the steering wheel. She could feel the tightness in her jaw and the heat of potential tears behind her eyes.

"Right after I moved home, he filed for divorce and pretty much had me evicted. His attorney got an order that I couldn't take the girls with me. They made it sound like I was unstable because I moved out and then back in. So the judge gave him custody."

The cowboy shrugged. "It's sort of surprising that the judge didn't see through that."

She sighed. "Well Keith had a terrific lawyer, Darrell Watkins. He somehow managed to take everything about my life and make me look unfit—or at least inept. Like, we had a couple court dates and both times they worked it so I had to come straight from my nursing practicals—so I was in my scrubs. I'm sure the judge thought that was a little disrespectful. And I didn't help my cause. I didn't have any lawyer and when Keith's attorney started pressing me, I would break down crying—like I always do when the stress gets to be too much. So they managed to make me look helpless and hopeless. I'm sure the judge thought the girls would be better off with their dad."

"Who was this judge?" he asked.

"Wheeler. Judge Thomas Wheeler. . . . Why do you ask?"

"I know him. Actually pretty well."

"Did you go through a divorce?

44

"No. No woman in her right mind would marry a rodeo cowboy, *Azulita*. I know him and I know of that lawyer, Darrell Watkins, because my dad is a lawyer. He has been since before I was born. I grew up knowing most of the law dogs, attorneys and judges in Tarrant County."

"Oh."

"But how have your girls been doing since they moved in with your ex?"

The tears began to flow again. LT turned his head to face the street and waited as Lisa tried to compose herself.

". . . I know they are clean and well-fed. They don't seem to be very happy, but maybe that's just the mom in me being overly sensitive. When I do get to see them, I try not to quiz them too much. I don't want them to doubt or criticize their dad just because of what he did to me."

"Well that's . . . I guess I'd say it's noble of you. He wouldn't ever hit them or neglect them, would he?"

She shook her head. "No. It's not physical with him. He just yells when he gets mad. He dominates people. As long as the girls stay quiet and submissive, he just sort of lets them be."

"Hmm. As a hospital social worker once said to me, that doesn't sound like much of a nurturing environment."

"Well there is a mother figure. Sort of. Shelli, the girl he left me for, moved in about the time he kicked me out. I think she tries to be there for the girls the best she can, even though I don't think she has much in the way of maternal instinct."

He glanced at her skeptically. "Judge Wheeler just let that co-habitation with minor children just slide?"

"Keith denied it. I tried to say he evicted me so they could live together. His lawyer said I was totally making it up, that I was grasping at straws to cover up my own inabilities." She turned down a street into an old neighborhood of small homes. "This is where I live."

He nodded. "Well I'll just sit out in the truck and be a gentleman and wait for you to change. Only, don't change too much."

She smiled as she parked his truck in the short, narrow drive in front of her rent house. "I'll hurry."

"Take your time." He produced a cell phone. "I need to make a couple phone calls anyway."

Lisa let herself into the house and scurried around the living room, picking up the dishes and nursing text books she had left lying in disarray from the night before. It was a strange thing to do, she told herself, since the cowboy was waiting for her. She was afraid, she realized, that he might come inside while she was dressing and see that her house was a mess. He might think the judge was right to let her ex have custody of Nita and Nelly.

Another part of her, though, wanted him to come into her house. The thought of making love to him in her own bed filled Lisa with electric excitement. It dawned on her that she had never made love in this little house—in fact, had not made love since the last time she had been with Keith. And if they were going to see LT's friends, apparently that meant they would not make love today. Did he not want her that way? What if the cowboy had not been as aroused, thrilled and sated by their coupling as she had been?

She pulled on her favorite blue jeans and a western shirt over a sleeveless t-shirt. As she forced her feet down into her riding-heel boots, she wondered if indeed she would go riding this day. The last thing she grabbed before heading out of the bedroom was the straw cowboy hat from the top shelf in her little closet.

LT was still talking on the phone as she opened the driver's door and slide into the pickup. He was listening intently and nodding his head.

"Thank you, Claudia," he said. "It would mean the world to me if it could happen tomorrow. . . . Yes ma'am. And I do thank you." He pushed a button on the phone and dropped it into his shirt pocket. "Look at you, cowgirl. Can't tell if you're ready to go rodeoing or line dancing."

She leaned toward him and said, "I haven't been to a lot of

rodeos. And I haven't been dancing in five or six years."

"Yeah, well, I bet you still have a step or two you could show me. Back on out of here and let's go get on I-30."

It was a half-mile drive from the country road down the gravel pathway to the ranch. Lisa could see the spread all the way: three good sized houses, a large barn and half a dozen corrals—plus the pasture, stretching beyond her vision and marked by a white three rail fence.

"All this is yours?"

"Yeah, I guess it is."

"And you have cows?"

"No." He chuckled. "Well yes. I have a few head I need to practice calf roping and steer wrangling. Now those really belong to Felipe. He runs a couple dozen head of Herefords. Me? I raise mostly horses."

She glanced at him. "How many do you have?"

"Now? Well . . . I just sold a few I had been training. So, sixty maybe."

She gasped. "You have sixty horses?"

He looked at her. "That ain't a lot. Only a dozen or so are cutting horses—you know, like I use in the rodeo. The rest are quarter horses."

"Quarter horses?"

"Yeah. Race horses, you know." He shrugged. "I'm too big to be a jockey, but I can still raise 'em and train 'em. Rodeo doesn't go on all the time. I got to have something to do in the off season."

". . . Oh."

"It's just a hobby. I'm lucky to break even at it. Well, I've been pretty lucky, so I guess I've done a little better than break even."

"You're pretty good at everything you try," she said. "At least it seems that way to me."

LT smiled slyly. "I'll take that as a compliment. Just pull up in front of the big house yonder."

The largest of the houses was brick and frame, a dusty brown with pale, dark green trim that seemed to match the Texas prairie stretching out all around the ranch. As she pulled to the head of the drive and stopped, a small black and white dog soared past the front of the vehicle, circled around and came to a stop by the driver's door. It was, she saw as she got out of the truck, a border collie. The dog cocked its head to one side, confused to see this stranger getting out the white truck.

"Rocket!" LT had pushed open the passenger's door. "Come here, boy."

Instantly the dog disappeared. Lisa saw it again as she walked around the back of the truck and looked at the cowboy sitting in the pickup and the door leaping into the air before him repeatedly, seeming to beg him to get out and play.

"Okay, okay," LT said. "Just give me a minute."

The dog stopped jumping and sniffed the protruding cast. Lisa lifted the crutches out of the bed of the truck and handed them to LT.

"Hello."

Coming from the barn toward them was an Hispanic man in his forties. He wore cowboy attire as well, though she suspected his clothes—unlike hers— were more about function than fashion.

"Lisa Newsome, meet Felipe Garza. Felipe, Lisa is *mi amiga nueva*."

"Nice to meet you."

"*Mucho gusto, senorita*," Felipe said. He turned to LT. "*Te tiene razón, ella es realmente muy bonito*."

"What?"

"Oh, Felipe said you look sort of silly wearing boots and a hat when you're clearly a city girl."

The rancher laughed. "That's not what I said at all," he responded in perfect English. "LT told me you were a pretty miss and I was just telling him that he was right."

"Aren't all the girls he brings out here pretty?"

Felipe shook his head. "You are the first *dama* to come here

48

in a very long time, Miss Newsome. And by far the most beautiful."

Lisa stood staring, wondering what to say. "May I call you Felipe? And would you call me Lisa?"

He gave a little bow. "I would be honored to do so."

LT, who had been leaning on his crutches petting the dog and listening to the conversation, spoke up. "And this here is Rocket."

She held out her hand for the Border Collie to sniff. "Is he your dog or Felipe's?"

"No. I reckon he's pretty much a ranch hand, just like the rest of us. Works as hard as any of us, doesn't he, *hombre*?"

"*Si*," Felipe said. "He brings in the cattle and ponies at night. Warns us of bobcats, coyotes and snakes."

"Snakes?"

"Oh hello! Hello!"

It was the voice of a woman. She was coming from the open garage of the house—a Latina wearing a light blue dress and welcoming smile. As Lisa held out her hand, the woman embraced her, hugging her tightly.

"You are Miss Lisa, the nurse of our LT?" Her face was full of delight.

"Yes. Yes. And you are Constan—"

"Constanza Garza." Now she grasped Lisa's hand. "I'm so glad to meet you, to thank you personally for taking such loving care of our friend."

The remembered image of them crying out in ecstasy as they made ravenous love flashed through her mind.

"He's an easy patient. If I get stern with him, he does what I say."

Constanza put her hands on her hips. "Well I'm so glad to hear that. He does nothing anyone else tells him."

"It's that needle she uses to give me my medicine," LT said. "If I back sass her, she says she'll give me the shot in a bad place while I'm sleeping. I'm scared to cross her."

"Right." Constanza's voice was skeptical. "I got your lunch ready."

"Lunch," Lisa responded. "It's not even ten yet."

"Oh I figured we'd go for a little ride. Up over the north hills yonder. It'll be dinner time when we get there and I thought we could stop and have a picnic."

Felipe nodded. "The ponies are saddled and ready."

"Ride on horses? Wow, cowboy, you never said anything about that. You can't go riding with your leg yet."

"*Azulita*, the horse ain't on me. I'm on the horse."

"Still—"

"Senorita," Felipe interrupted, "*Gallo* has done this with broken bones many times before. He won't listen to any of us who tell him not to."

"See," LT said. "And I do just fine, don't I, *hombre*."

Felipe shook his head. He turned to Lisa. "I think riding is part of the cure for him."

". . . You mean, part of the patient's healing process?"

The rancher nodded. "As you say, senorita. I'll bring up the horses."

"Yes," Constanza said, "and I'll bring your lunch. It's packed."

The dog dashed toward the barn when it realized where Felipe was going. So for a moment it was just the nurse and the cowboy standing by the truck, gazing at the vast prairie around them.

She looked at LT. "I dont think there is a cure for you."

"I'm not sure how you mean that."

"I could mean a couple things, couldn't I? Are you a breaker of hearts, Mr. LT?" She sighed as she took in the vista before them. "It's hard for me to get my mind around the idea that all of this is yours."

He smile and gave the slightest shrug. "You ever heard that song 'Oklahoma'? There's a line in there: 'They know they belong to the land and the land they belong to is grand.' I think that's the way it is with me. Sometimes, especially when I camp out at night by myself, I think that I belong to the wilderness. It's like . . . this little piece of Texas has trusted itself to me."

For the first half hour of their ride across the prairie she concentrated on following closely behind the cowboy, and reacquainting herself with the feel and balance of riding a horse. Trixie, the paint mare to whom they had entrusted her, seemed to have things under control. As promised, she was a placid horse who had no objection to a strange, slightly anxious rider.

In the second half hour she began to pay attention to the land they were crossing: the capricious hills, dry creek beds, random stands of mesquite trees and blossoms of fat, round cacti. To Lisa there was no distinct trail, though LT seemed to know exactly where he was going.

By the end of the first hour, she had accumulated a number of questions she yearned to ask him. Summoning her courage, she urged Trixie forward to ride alongside the cowboy.

He glanced toward her casually. "Howdy."

"I have a couple questions."

"Oh yeah?"

"What was that name Felipe called you?"

"You mean *Gallo*? That's Spanish for . . . rooster."

She smiled. "Okay. Who lives in which house?"

"Whenever I'm not rodeoing or recuperating, I live in the big house. Constanza keeps up both houses. They live in the smaller one with a couple of their kids. And the third one is a guest house. . . . Although I don't have many guests."

"Was Felipe telling the truth about you not bringing other girls to your farm?"

"Yeah, I guess. Course I've only lived here for eight or ten years."

"Why haven't you brought your girlfriends out here? You can't tell me you don't have rodeo 'groupies'."

He gazed her wryly, deciding how to respond. "I got a broken leg, *Azulita*. I'd be stupid not to bring along a nurse for my first ride back in the saddle."

She smiled. "That's a clever dodge. I'm not asking why you

51

brought me. I'm asking why you haven't brought others." She cocked her head. "You must've had your heart broken."

"Ha. I had my heart broke by my 'true love' when I was sixteen. Within a couple weeks I began to realize how lucky I was. Since then I've been rather cautious about trusting my poor, innocent heart to a lady."

"That's strange—the idea of you being so cautious. You are the biggest daredevil I've ever known. Do you trust me?"

"I do, actually."

"Why?"

"Well. When you first met me you had no idea who I was. The way you treated me—the way you still treat me—has nothing to do with me being a world champion cowboy. Well I was. A couple times. Hope to be world champion again. To you, I was the patient you invested your caring in. . . . And then, well, you are sort of a knock out."

"A knock out? . . . Are you just teasing me?"

He laughed. "And then there's that. You don't seem to have any idea what a looker you are, or what a killer personality you have." He nodded. "You see that stand of cottonwoods?"

"Uh. I don't know one tree from another."

"Oh." He chuckled. "Well you see that low place up ahead surrounded by the trees with the bright green leaves. I figured that's where we'd stop for our picnic."

The little oasis he described seemed to arise mystically from the scrubby flatland. A creek ran away from the trees and the horses plodded in the shallow, clear water.

"It's so pretty."

"Yes. This is . . . well I guess this is my favorite place anywhere. The water is from a spring underground. Cottonwoods grow along streams and they make for a lot of interesting shade and cover from the wind and rain. And bunches of different little critters come to drink here. . . . As pretty as it is during the day, it's amazingly beautiful at night. Especially when there is no moon. The Milky Way shines enough light that you can see anything move, even way off in the distance."

"You come out here at night?"

"Me and Rex camp out here often as we can."

"Just you and your horse?"

"Ssh. Rex don't know he's a horse. Yeah, me and the pony. Sometimes Rocket comes along, but he don't like that I won't let him chase the coyotes."

"Why won't you let him chase coyotes?"

He looked at her. "Because they're pack hunters. They'll lure him out and surround him. He's plenty fast, but they'll cut him off and have him for supper."

"Oh."

He stopped beneath the cottonwoods. "This is our spot. Just let your reins drop and you can get off."

"Won't she—"

"No, Trixie will stand and let you dismount."

She sat in the saddle watching nervously as LT dismounted, sliding his cast over Rex's back and lifting his leg, then pulling his boot out of the stirrup and sliding to the ground. He looked up at Lisa and laughed.

"I didn't know how you were going to do that without rebreaking your leg. And then I didn't know what I was going to do."

"Hey, this ain't my first rodeo. If I was able, I'd help you down, but—"

"No, no. I got this."

Gingerly she lifted her right leg and lowered herself to the ground. She listened as he gave her instructions for securing the horses. He had brought his crutches in a rifle scarab on his saddle and leaned on them as he pulled opened the leather pouches on the saddle and began to take out the spread of food Constanza had packed their for lunch.

"You see that blanket tied behind your saddle?" he said. "Would you take that to the high side of the creek in that grassy spot and open it up for us?"

She expected it to be a dusty horse blanket, but found instead it was soft, new braided material that smelled a little like straw. When Lisa spread it, she was surprised at how large it was, and how inviting. She sat down on the edge of it almost reverently and slipped off her boots and hat. She ran her hand across it, reveling in the unexpected hospitality of it.

It dawned on her that she sensed no noise or movement from LT. When she turned toward the creek, she saw him leaning on his crutches, picnic food in hand, watching her silently.

"It's so . . . nice just to sit here on the blanket."

Wordlessly he set the bundle down and dropped his hat and crutches on the ground. He lowered himself to the blanket and scooted to her side.

"Could you help me with my boot, *Azulita*?"

She bent the toe back toward him and slid the boot off and tossed it beside hers. Lying on his back, propped up on his elbows, he gazed at her.

"May I kiss you?" he asked.

"I wish you would, cowboy."

He put a hand behind her head and pulled her to him, giving her a long, sweet, electric kiss that immediately brought to mind the first kiss he had given her the day before. When he leaned back to breathe, he held her close.

"I been waiting all these years to find someone I wanted to share this spot with."

". . . What a beautiful thing to say."

"Well you're a beautiful lady."

He gave her another kiss and, as he did, she pushed him flat on the ground and lay astride him. Pressing her lips to his, she pulled his shirt from his jeans and ran her hand up along his lean chest, pinching his nipple. And he responded by finding the bottom of her t-shirt and slipping his hands—hard and strong, but not rough—against her skin. He pushed her shirt upward until he came to her bra. Gently he forced it up and over her breasts and lowered her chest onto his.

"Ah." He closed his eyes. "Will you make love to me, *Azulita*?"

Sliding her hand down inside his jeans, she grasped his cock, already beginning to stiffen.

"I thought you'd never ask."

LT put his hands on her hips and pushed, sliding jeans and panties together down over her bottom. And as he did, she undid his belt and pants opening the zipper. They pressed themselves to each other, his penis rock hard against her soft belly.

Lisa lifted herself up and pulled off his jeans and underwear completely. He had pinned the cut leg of his jeans loosely, so it slid easily over his cast. Then she lay on her back and pushed her own jeans and panties off her feet. For an instant they lay side by side, each naked from the waist down, staring at one another. Her eyes gravitated to his erect, slightly bent member.

"As a nurse I have to warn you that, even in the shade, a penis exposed to the sun can get a terrible sunburn."

"Hmm. I better cover it up then."

"I have a place for it."

She rolled over and straddled him, a knee on either side of his hips. Reaching behind and below, she grasped his dick. He tensed and moaned and then relaxed. Lisa lowered herself onto him, guiding the phallus deeply, slowly inside.

"You're very wet."

She leaned forward, her eyes closed, sighing. "You make me so wet."

He sucked her nipple into his mouth, circling the areola with his tongue, and simutaneously beginning to raise and lower his hips. She pressed her thighs against his hips to accentuate her awareness of the phallus rising and falling within her. And irresistibly she began to lift and lower herself. Their shared rocking motion was excruciatingly deliberate, as they paused at each peak and each valley. As she lifted herself, his member slipped out. The cowboy reached down for it and rubbed the hot head of it against her tender clitoris.

"Oh! God, LT."

She pressed her face to his, kissing him wantonly, forcing

55

her tongue into his mouth, sucking his, taut, into her mouth. Still holding their kiss, he entered her again, long and hard. Of their own accord, her inner lips tightened on him. She came, shivers running through her, the walls of her passage taut, gripping his member even as the rest of her body became flaccid and she collapsed onto him.

"Say, uh."

"Oh, did I stop at a bad time?"

"Well I am kind of at—a desperate point, if you know what I mean."

She kissed him, wet and forceful, squeezing his cock within her and holding it motionless. "So." Her voice was coy. "Where do you want me?"

The boyish grin creased his face. Instantly he rolled her off top of him, completely around so that her back was against his side. The movement was surprising, swift and delightful and even more so when he spread her legs, lifting one so it sat atop his hip and entered her, his front to her back. And once the penis sank within her, he remained still. Gradually he began to move again. She closed her eyes at the exquisite feeling of the shaft sliding within her vagina. And then she felt his hand reach over stomach and caress her clitoris and then run upward sweetly. She pressed herself down on his hand and his cock.

"Oh. Cowboy?"

"Yes, my love."

"You have to cum now."

"Right now?"

"Right now."

"But I'm enjoying this fucking so much."

"Oh-oh-oh-oh. . . . Never mind. Too late."

His rhythm increased quickly. "Great, *Azulita*. Now you got me all worked up. . . . Now I'm . . . ."

She felt the exertion, the upward reaching of his member as he came, moaning softly. He continued moving into and out of her for a full minute, until gradually his energy at last seemed spent. He lowered her leg and spooned tightly against her back, his hand firmly cupped over her breast. The texture of his palm over her aroused nipple caused her to catch her breath.

"You know—" Her voice was ragged. "—There is going to be a huge wet spot right in the middle of this blanket. It's probably going to leave a stain. And I don't think it will dry out by the time we get back."

"Probably not." He rolled onto his back. "Especially if I get what I want for dessert." He drew a deep breath. "I'll just tell Constanza we spilled the tea."

"You really think she'll believe that?"

He rolled his head over to look at her. "I have it on good authority that Felipe takes her on picnics too."

Chapter 4

She wasn't asleep when the phone rang. Lisa had been lying awake for half an hour, wavering between despair and hope.

She despaired of seeing her daughters anytime soon. Keith had essentially stolen them and was daring her to try to get them back. That fight would have to take place in a courtroom, an arena she had neither the money nor time to enter. It made her wonder when she would be able to spend time with Nita and Nelly again. Eventually, she speculated, Keith would tire of having them around and would send them back to her—with the caveat, she was sure, that he could pull them away on a whim.

Oddly, though, in another way she was also full of hope. Hope that perhaps the passionate relationship she had developed with the cowboy so swiftly might not end as abruptly as it had begun. And her thoughts, as she lay in her bed alone, swung from her daughters to her new lover.

He had leaned on his crutches and watched her get into her Honda the evening before, just after she had delivered him to his parents' home. His face was lit with affection.

"Say, *Azulita*," he had called before she could close the driver's door, "you think I could call you again? Even though you're not my nurse anymore."

"I would love it if you called me." She stared at him, wanting him to ask her to stay. "Is there anything you need before I go?"

He shook his head wearily. "I'm going to take some pain pills and go to sleep. I might have overdid it a little today."

She nodded. "'Overdone' it. And you definitely did. . . . Thank you for today, LT."

"You are as welcome as you can be. There's no way you could have enjoyed it any more than I did." He tilted his head. "Reckon I have to take you back to the farm soon. You were a real hit with Constanza and Felipe. I'll never hear the end of it if I don't bring you back."

". . . Just say when. If you need help with anything, call me. My card—it's by the phone in the kitchen."

His eyebrows arched momentarily. "I think I already know your number by heart."

But when the phone rang before 8 a.m. that Friday morning, it was not LT she expected to be calling. Perhaps, she hoped as she picked up her cell, it was Keith saying he had changed his mind, that the girls were going to be hers for the weekend.

"Hello?"

"*Azulita?*"

"LT, how are you? Do you need me? I mean, are you having some trouble?"

"No, I'm pretty good today. I need to make another little trip and I sure would appreciate it if you'd take me."

"Another trip?" She sat up in bed. "You really do push the envelope. After that long ride yesterday, I think you should take a couple days and just rest."

"Well I ain't got as far to go today. But I need you to come along if you will."

She sighed. She loved spending time with the cowboy. And she didn't mind looking out for him. After three twelve-hour days, she was supposed to have at least two days off—not to mention she had emptied her weekend work schedule in anticipation of being with her girls.

"Okay, rodeo boy. Somebody has to keep an eye on you. Where are we going and when?"

"Just downtown Ft. Worth. But we need to be there at 9 a.m."

She swung around to look at the clock. "Christ, LT, it's 7:45. No way do I have time to get ready, get to your house and have you downtown by 9."

"Well what if you didn't have to come to my house?"

"What?"

"I'm sitting in your driveway."

After an instant's hesitation, she shut off the phone and slid out of bed. She lumbered sleepily out of the bedroom through the living room to the front door. Pulling it open part way and peaking around it, she gazed into the bright morning sunlight. Sure enough, the dusty white pickup sat behind her Honda in the driveway. When he saw her, the cowboy, sitting behind the steering wheel, lifted a small white paper sack and a drink carrier. She stuck her arm outside the door and motioned for him to come into the house.

It took a minute for him to clamber out, fish his crutches out of the bed of the truck and, holding the sack in his teeth and balancing the drink carrier precariously, make his way to her front door. She took the bag and tray from him and closed the door behind him.

"How is it you can drive when you aren't supposed to put any weight on your cast?"

He grinned the wily, boyish grin that she loved—but which filled her with apprehension. "Turns out I'm ambi-dexterious with my feet. I propped my right leg on the passenger's side and drove with my left foot." He glanced about himself. "So this is your place. Pretty nice." He held the drink carrier toward her." I don't know if you start off with coffee or orange juice, so I got both."

"Coffee, please."

"And I brought fresh donuts."

"Donuts! Do you know how fattening those are?"

"Well, we got to put back on you what we wore off yesterday."

"Right. You could give a girl a heads up, you know. Instead of just coming over unannounced—with just an hour to get you where you have to be."

He gazed at her as she stood before him, her breasts free and resplendent beneath her sheer summer nightie. "Well here's the deal. I figured if I showed up any earlier or gave us anymore time, instead of getting ready for our excursion, I would have succumbed to your feminine delights again and missed my appointment altogether."

"Appointment? Oh. I have to jump in the shower."

He nodded. "Not that you offered for me to come along, but the smartest thing—if we're not going to be late—is for me to wait right here."

"I'll hurry."

He smiled. "I'll wait, little blue eyes."

He didn't argue when she insisted on driving. He seemed completely comfortable with his shoulder pressed against her and his leg on seat. And on this second day of driving it, Lisa felt acclimated to the truck. They backed out of the driveway and started toward downtown.

"Where exactly are we going?"

"Courthouse. The county courthouse." He looked at her. "You know how to get there, right?"

"Oh yes. Scene of my greatest misery and defeat. . . . Why do you need to go there? You suing the bull who broke your leg?"

"It was a bronc did that. Six or eight months from now I'm going to meet up with that pony again."

"You're not going to hurt him, are you?"

"Only his dignity. Horse's name is Kodiak. That was only the second time I ever drew him. I was about to make it to the bell. Know what that means?"

"Uh, not really."

"Well, in the riding events you're supposed to stay up on the bull or the horse for eight seconds. When you hear the bell, you jump off. . . . I was going to make the full ride. I knew it and Kodiak knew it. That's why he put me into the wall."

"You make it sound like he knew what he was doing."

He smiled broadly. "He knew exactly what he was doing. And I guarantee when I get back on him next spring, he will remember me."

She considered his words silently. "I didn't think the horse

61

ever saw who was riding him."

"That's true, unless you intentionally get down before the ride and look 'em in the eye like some of the fellows do. But you really don't have to do that. They know you if you have history with 'em regardless. It's not my face he'll recognize. I don't know how they know who's ridin' 'em. Smell maybe. The way you feel on their backs. Or maybe how you cinch down. But they know. And I'd know him with my eyes closed, sure enough."

Doubt creased her face. "How you going to keep him from crushing you on the fence again?"

LT nodded. "He jumps and bucks once, twice, then spins left all the way around. Then he starts again: buck, buck, spin left. He turns left because most of us hold with our left hands. Makes it hard to brace yourself. Only when he comes out of that second jump, I'm cross yanking his head to the right. It's going to straighten him up and send him back to bucking. And either it will keep him centered in the ring or he'll fall over to his side."

". . . Sounds like you've been thinking about this a lot."

"All the way home laying on the seat of the truck with the bone sticking out and my leg throbbing. You bet that sweet, round, little ass of yours I thought about him plenty." He turned to her. "Did I just insult you?"

"I didn't take it that way. Now if you said, 'You bet your great big behind,' it might have hurt my feelings."

He chuckled. "Well, I'm sorry if I said something ugly. Sure didn't mean to."

"You never did say why you're going to the courthouse."

"I got an appointment with a lawyer friend of mine. Betty Kupchek. She's conducting a little legal procedure for me. I'll introduce you. You'll like her. Family law is her specialty."

"Really. I bet she's expensive."

"Ah, they're all expensive. But some of them are worth it. Betty is amazing. My dad says she's a miracle worker. Just having her on your case makes the other side want to settle."

He popped open the glove box and pulled out a blue handicapped tag. Lisa stared at him as he hooked it around the rearview mirror.

"I got it after my last go-round with the saw bones. You know, directly in front of the main courthouse door is a handicap parking lot."

"Okay."

He seemed to grow quiet then, watching the flow of traffic thoughtfully as she made her way through the city. For her part, she wondered what kind of legal action was bringing him to the courthouse. Despite the intimacy they had shared, there was so much about him she didn't know.

LT actually held the door for her as they entered the courthouse, though he remained silent as they walked through the bustling corridors and entered the elevator. Punching the "4" button, he leaned against the back of the elevator and sighed. He looked at his watch.

"Almost 9. We made good time. Betty's supposed to be up here waiting."

Lisa nodded. "I remember that the fourth floor is all courtrooms. Should I wait out in the hall for you?"

"Oh no," he replied quickly. "I expect you need to come in with me."

". . . Okay."

The elevator door rolled open slowly and they started down the hallway. Judge Wheeler's courtroom, Lisa knew, was at the end of this hallway. Her heart fluttered and her face flushed at the remembrance of the disaster that had overwhelmed her there.

A somewhat stout, professionally dressed, pleasant-looking women in her 50s stood in front of the doors to Judge Wheeler's courtroom. As they approached, she beamed a matronly smile toward LT.

"Hi, Betty."

"Good morning, Mr. Tolliver. How are you?"

"If I was any better, I couldn't stand it. And this is—"

"Hello," the lawyer extended her hand. "You must be Lisa Newsome."

She was stunned. Grasping Betty's hand, she wasn't sure how to respond.

"Uh. Uh. You must be Miss Kup—"

"Kupchek." She smiled. "Yes I am. Are you ready? I think they're ready for us."

"Ready?"

"Uh, Betty," the cowboy said, "I didn't exactly tell Lisa what was going to happen this morning. You know, in case you couldn't pull everything together."

The attorney placed her face alongside LT's—her mouth at his ear—and, with a charming smile, said, "You little shit. I can't believe you would bring her up here without explaining what was going on." She turned to Lisa. "Miss Newsome, Judge Wheeler has graciously granted us an emergency child protective custody hearing for your children Anita and Nellie."

"What?" She felt for an instant that she would wet her pants. "Are the girls okay? Did something happen to them? Did I do something wrong?"

"Not you, sweetie," Betty said. "You're children are just fine. Let's go on in here and see what happens."

The attorney pulled open the courtroom doors and hastened through with an air of great confidence. Following her, in uncertainty and utter confusion, was Lisa. Hobbling behind them on his crutches came LT.

A loud, vaguely familiar voice was the first thing to impress itself on Lisa's senses. The voice, she realized quickly, belonged to Darrell Watkins, the attorney who had utterly humiliated her during the custody hearing. He was standing at the front of the courtroom, clenching a sheath of papers and speaking to Judge Thomas Wheeler in an extremely confrontational tone. Lisa stopped completely only a few steps from the entrance when she recognized her ex-husband standing beside his attorney, Keith's face a deep, furious red. Cold fear seized her—leavened immediately by hope. This was something the cowboy had set up. Maybe, if this lawyer was representing her, she would get to see the girls over the weekend after all.

And as she stood watching the bizarre scene unfold before her, she felt the nearby presence of someone else she knew. She turned to the row of seats on the back wall of the courtroom and saw Shelli Munroe—Keith's paramour, who had moved into Lisa's house and taken over the role of mother to her two daughters—sitting in silence. This day she was dressed in a conservative business-blue dress. She raised her eyes to Lisa and gave a shrug and a little smile.

"Yes, Mr. Watkins, I received the very same petition, which is why I called this emergency hearing." This was the judge speaking for the first time. And now he addressed the lawyer Lisa had just met in the hallway. "Ms. Kupchek, since you have gathered us all here on the spur of the moment—when this is not a court day for me, I assume you can demonstrate the urgent need for a protective order?"

Betty Kupchek's manner and voice were disarmingly casual as she pulled documents from a leather briefcase. "Yes, your honor. The plaintiff has three concerns. We not only assert but can demonstrate clearly, first, that Mr. Newsome has routinely defied the court's directives and arbitrarily prevented Mrs. Newsome's daughters from seeing their mother."

"Routinely?" the judge said.

"Yes, your honor."

Judge Wheeler scowled. "Just how routinely?" He looked at Keith. "Have you been denying your children the privilege of seeing their mother without the court's permission?"

"Your Honor—" Keith began.

"My client may have had to change his schedule a time or two," his attorney interrupted. "This resulted in having to reschedule the visitation—"

"Mrs. Newsome." The judge looked out at Lisa, who was still straggling toward the front of the courtroom.

"Hello, your Honor."

"In the six months since I granted him custodial custody, how many times has your husband refused to allow your daughters their regular bi-weekly visitation?"

She nodded. "Seven times since he took them, your Honor. Not counting this weekend, which would make eight."

The room was quiet as the judge looked over his glasses at her. "And why is it in particular that he won't allow you to visit your daughters this weekend, Mrs. Newsome."

"He said it was inconvenient, your Honor."

Keith's attorney spoke up immediately. "This is semantics, Your Honor. I can assure you my client would never attempt to suborn the court's—"

The judge extended his hand like a stop sign. "Just a minute, counselor. I'd like to hear from Mr. Newsome why it is inconvenient to obey my custody decree."

It was the first time in her life that Lisa had seen Keith speechless. His complexion visibly went from dark red to chalky gray. His mouth open, he searched for how to respond.

"Your Honor?" It was Betty Kupchek who broke the silence. "Not to interrupt, but Mr. Newsome's disregard of the court's visitation ruling is the least of the plaintiff's concerns."

"Do tell," the judge said.

"We are gravely concerned about the welfare, nurture and development of these children while in the care of Mr. Newsome."

Lisa was suddenly very interested in what Betty was saying. Was this just a legal ploy, or was Keith really mistreating her girls?

"Proceed."

The attorney—her attorney, she was beginning to feel—stepped in front of the elevated bench and set several documents before Judge Wheeler. As she began to speak again, her face and voice remarkably tranquil, she handed copies to Darrell Watkins as well.

"I present to the court three affidavits: one from the principal of the school attended last semester by the Newsome children; one from Anita's teacher and one from Nellie's teacher. You'll see that each of these women expressed real concern about the marked change in the girls' behavior. Throughout the year they became noticeably more withdrawn. Their grades suffered. They ceased interacting with the other children."

Lisa felt her face flush. Her jaw dropped. She turned toward Keith.

"This is subjective and hearsay, Your Honor." Watkin's voice was sharp and defensive. "It's quite normal for children to have adverse reactions when they go through a contested divorce. Not to be chauvinistic, Your Honor, but it's very likely these teachers had a relationship with my client's ex-wife and therefore resented the children's father when he, rightfully, gained full custody. If these teachers and the principal had concerns about the well-being of the girls, they should have brought it to the attention of their father."

"They did," Betty said curtly. "As the affidavits attest, Your Honor, the principal requested a meeting with Mr. Newsome when he ignored repeated requests from the teachers for conferences about the girls. Mr. Newsome was not willing to meet."

Her voice low with anger and hurt, Lisa whispered to Keith. "What have you done to my babies?"

"Ms. Kupchek," the judge said, "if they couldn't manage to get a conference with the father, why didn't they ask to meet with Mrs. Newsome."

Betty's face was emotionless. "Because, as the affidavits state, Mr. Newsome told the principal that the plaintiff had abandoned her daughters and that her whereabouts were unknown."

"You bastard!"

There was flat slapping sound as the judge's gavel struck the bench before him. It made Lisa stop and breathe. In that instant, she realized everyone in the courtroom was standing except for the judge, Shelli at the back and LT, who was sitting silently in the row behind the plaintiff's desk. His eyes, full of power and patience, met hers.

"All right, everyone have a seat and let's see if we can sort this out."

"Your Honor?" It was Betty Kupchek once again, now the only one who was standing. "We have not yet stated the plaintiff's major concern."

Judge Wheeler gazed at her warily. "Please proceed, Ms. Kupchek."

"Your Honor, as your custody decree attests, you found the plaintiff to be unstable and unreliable. You were led to these conclusions because Mr. Newsome—" She glanced at him. "—perjured himself in sworn testimony. We are prepared to demonstrate the truth of the situation. As she testified before you, Mrs. Newsome initially took her daughters and moved out of their home when Mr. Newsome would not. She felt compelled to leave her husband because he was involved in an adulterous affair.

"He deceived her into returning to their home by telling her the affair was over when in point of fact it was not. It was from the beginning his intention to have the children brought back to the home and then force the plaintiff by court order to leave— which his attorney sought and you granted—and gain the upper hand in the subsequent custody case. Further, Mr. Newsome lied to you under oath when he said he was not engaged in an extra-marital relationship. He did in point of fact move the correspondent, Ms. Shelli Munroe into the residence within twenty-four hours of taking custody of the children."

Watkins got to his feet, shaking his head. "Your Honor, this is a he said-she said dispute. My client had no need or desire to offer anything but the whole truth in the aforesaid custody hearing. We would point out that the plaintiff's attorney has no evidence to support her inflammatory claims."

Judge Wheeler cut his eyes to Betty. "Well, Mrs. Kupchek, can you substantial these claims? You have more affidavits, do you?"

"No, your Honor. I have a witness who can confirm all these facts." She motioned toward the back of the courtroom. "I would like to swear in Miss Shelli Munroe, the correspondent in question and former live-in girlfriend of Mr. Newsome."

"Former?" Lisa whispered.

The judge looked at the young brunette seated by the exit. "Come forward, ma'am."

He nodded to a uniformed officer, who moved toward the bench. All watched in silence as the lithe, elegant woman walked to the front. She exuded a confident sexuality despite the diffident swiftness of her steps.

The bailiff raised a hand, to which Shelli responded by raising hers. "Do you swear to tell the truth, the whole truth and nothing but the truth under penalty of law?"

"I do."

"State your name."

"Shelli Marie Munroe."

The deputy faded to the edges of the courtroom. The judge gazed down at the new witness.

"If you'll permit me, Ms. Kupchek, I'd like to ask the questions. . . . Miss Munroe, were you in fact involved in a sexual relationship at the time of the hearing six months ago when custody of the Newsome children was awarded to Mr. Newsome?"

"Yes, your Honor."

The judge gave a weary nod. "And did you in fact move into the Newsome home within twenty-four hours after the conclusion of that hearing?"

She shrugged. "Yes and no, Your Honor. For all intents and purposes I was already living in the house before Keith got custody of the girls. When the court date was over and Keith won, I just moved the rest of my clothes in and officially gave up my apartment."

"Are you still living with Mr. Newsome and the children?

"No."

Judge Wheeler arched his eyebrows. "I take it the magic

69

went out of the relationship?"

". . . I'm not sure what you mean, Your Honor."

"Why did you move out?"

"Keith told me to get out."

"Really," Judge Wheeler said slowly. Watkins rose to speak, but the judge motioned for him to be seated without looking at him. "How is it that Mr. Newsome demanded that you leave his home?"

"I suppose it was a culmination of a number of things. Eventually there was a lot anger between us, Your Honor, beginning when he started calling me names and saying the same ugly things to me he used to say to Lisa."

Doubt flashed across the judge's face. "How would you know what ugly things Mr. Newsome said to Mrs. Newsome?"

"Because I heard him say them."

". . . When was this?"

"Before she left him. Before she knew about me. He would tell her he was working late, then he would come over to my apartment and we would make love. When we were through, he liked to lay in my bed and call her on his cell phone and tell her how hard he had to work and how she didn't appreciate him and how ungrateful she was and how unattractive she had become and what a lousy lover and wife she was. And all the time he was lying naked with me, fondling my breasts and my privates and making sure I stayed quiet. He loved to have control over the both of us at the same time."

Lisa watched Judge Wheeler's jaw clench and unclench. She had to focus on something, she realized, in order to deal with the surreal things the witness was saying.

"After I had lived with him and the girls about three or four months, he started saying those same things to me." She shrugged. "It was like he forgot that I heard him say all those things to Lisa. And it got worse between us when I began to criticize him for the way he treated the girls."

"What way was he treating them?"

She shook her head. "He bullied them. He refused to let

them visit their friends and absolutely refused to allow other girls to come visit Nita and Nellie. Every part of their lives was regulated. It was—it was just according to his whim at any given moment. It was—"

"Capricious and arbitrary?"

"Yes. It was that. And after that I discovered he was cheating on me the way he cheated on Lisa. I was home taking care of his children and he was out f— having sex with other women."

"And what made you think he was unfaithful to you, Miss Munroe?"

Shelli tilted her head to one side. "Well when he gave me venereal disease, that was pretty much a dead giveaway."

"He gave you VD?"

She nodded slowly. "Gonorrhea and chlamydia." In the moment of silence that followed, a tear traced down one of her cheeks, though she did not lose her composure. "And then he fired me."

There was an incredulous tone in the judge's voice. "You worked for him and he fired you from your job?"

"Yes, your Honor. It wasn't actually him. It was one of his underlings, Mr. Carliss. Poor little man is about two years from retirement. I knew what happened. If Carliss didn't fire me, Keith would have fired him."

This time Watkins leaped to his feet, only to be silenced again by the judge's outstretched hand.

"Miss Munroe, if Mr. Newsome was doing all these things to you, why did he have to tell you to leave? Seems to me you would have left on your own."

Her head dropped. "It was the girls, Your Honor. As long as I was in the house, there were limits to how mean he could be to them. And—" Tears began to flow. Her chin quivered. "—after how I contributed to Lisa losing her girls, I felt responsible to watch out for them as much as I could."

The judge sighed and looked down at the bench before him. He began to write in silence. Lisa remembered he done that

71

during the previous hearing just before he awarded custody of the girls to Keith. She held her breath. Apparently Darrell Watkins also realized what the judge was doing. With an expression of alarm, he got to his feet once more.

His voice had a forced calmness to it as he spoke. "Your Honor, none of this testimony has been substantiated. It is strictly the word of a would-be lover whose hopes for a long term relationship didn't work out. I would point out that my client and I have not had an opportunity to review and respond to these spurious attacks on his character."

"I am well-aware that this has not been substantiated, Mr. Watkins. That's why I am going to bring in our friends from the Department of Human Resources and let their social workers determine whether or not—as I suspect—everything Miss Munroe just said is true." He looked down at the witness. "Thank you for your testimony, miss. You may be dismissed."

As she turned to leave the courtroom, Shelli stopped at the plaintiff's desk. She grasped Lisa's hand for an instant, her face contorted with tears about to spill. Then she hurried down the aisle and out the door.

"Mr. Watkins."

"Yes, your Honor."

"Is there anything your client would like to say?"

Everyone in the courtroom turned to Keith. His mouth dropped open and, momentarily he uttered a single vowel. "Uh . . ."

"Your Honor," Watkins began swiftly, "we look forward to examining the complaint and responding to each assertion in such a way as to demonstrate my client's veracity and his worthiness as a parent. We are grateful for the court's wisdom and foresight in trusting the care of the Newsome children to their father."

The judge, looking down and writing again, nodded slowly. "Yes, Mr. Watkins, you are seeking to affix blame for this sorry situation on my judgment." He looked up at the attorney. "I would just say that, at the time I awarded custody to him,

Mr. Newsome could have chosen to be an ideal parent. Or he could have decided to be a jackass. Human Resources will help us make that determination. In your personal reflections on this, counselor, you might remember that you helped persuade me to make the custody decision. For future reference, I urge you to remember you are a successful attorney. You might do a better job of picking just who you'll be a hired gun for. Eh?"

He turned his attention to Lisa. "Mrs. Newsome?" She started to rise. "No, no. Keep your seat." He drew a deep breath. "There is a saying, Mrs. Newsome: the wheels of justice grind slow, but fine. I suspect in this case that means it has taken the court a while to determine the truth of your family situation. Of course, we do have to verify what has been said, today, though it does have the ring of truth to it—and it confirms what you testified at our first hearing.

"So here is what will happen next. The Department of Human Resources will commence an investigation. It will be quite thorough, though I suspect it will not be terribly intrusive into your life. You can expect this will take several months. As the conclusion, you will be notified as to the results of the investigation. I may request that you come back to meet with me. Or maybe not.

"In the meantime, I would like you to go over to Mr. Newsome's home this evening and collect your daughters and their possessions. Would a five p.m. deadline give you adequate time to have your home ready for your daughters?"

"Oh yes, Your Honor."

"The court awards custody of Anita and Nellie to you pending the findings of the DHR report. Mr. Newsome will be granted bi-weekly supervised visitation as established by the department." His eyebrows lifted and he smiled pleasantly. "Is there anything else, ma'am?"

"Thank you so much, Your Honor."

He nodded and slapped down the gavel once more. "We are adjourned."

Everyone but Keith rose as the judge swiftly got up and left through the door behind the bench. The two attorneys gathered their papers, stuffing them into their cases. Watkins smiled, in awe and admiration it seemed to Lisa.

"How long did it take you to pull this together, Betty?"

"Twenty-four hours."

"Get outa here. Twenty-four hours?"

"A lot of people seemed eager to talk about your client."

Lisa turned to LT, who had propped his crutches beneath his arms. He smiled at her and started toward the door. She was holding the exit open for him, trying to think of how to put the gratitude she was feeling into words, when Keith caught up with them.

"You think this is over, don't you, you little bitch?" His voice was low, but intense. "You think you can blindside me in a courtroom and get away with it?"

Lisa didn't respond. She had won and it wasn't necessary to speak to him. Replying to him would only perpetuate the awkward moment and fuel the rage he was feeling.

"And if you think I'm going to give you enough child support to pay for your goddamned high-dollar attorney, you're wrong."

LT was making his way as swiftly as he could to the elevators with Lisa right beside him. The attorneys apparently could hear the tone of Keith's voice and were trying to catch up with the three of them.

"I was easy on you the first time, Lisa. The next time we go through this, I promise, I will get your parental rights terminated. You'd better enjoy the next few weeks with the girls, because that's the end of you seeing them—ever."

She breathed a sigh of relief when the elevator door opened right away and LT hobbled inside and pushed the button for the ground floor. Lisa went to the back wall, looking away from her ex. Apparently not finished with his diatribe, Keith followed her in and stood above her, looking down at her as he continued.

"You think Wheeler is the only judge, little missy? He's

not. I can shop judges like you can shop lawyers."

The two attorneys got to the elevator door just as it was rolling closed. LT held up his hand and Betty Kupchek stopped. She grabbed Watkin's arm and pulled him to a stop as the door shut.

Oblivious to the descent of the elevator, Keith continued his rant. "And it seems to me you and Shelli are new best friends. Did the two of you harpies cook this whole thing up together? I should have known that she'd end up being as worthless and malicious as you are."

The elevator lurched and stopped moving. An alarm bell began to ring. Lisa looked to LT, who was standing motionless on his crutches, his back to the two of them. They had stopped halfway between the third and second floor.

"What the hell? What did you do?" Keith's voice was full of the same venom, but much louder as he spoke for the first time to LT. "Did you pull the emergency button, you scrawny, little redneck? Who the hell are you, anyway, you little shit?"

LT glanced over his shoulder at the tall, menacing figure at the back of the elevator and then looked back to the control panel.

"Do you not hear me, sonny? Start us up again right now before I break something you can't put in a cast."

Then came one of those startlingly fast movements Lisa had come to associate with cowboy's amazing physical abilities. The end of his right crutch flew backward between Keith's legs and made solid contact with his groin. There was the sound of air bursting from Keith's lungs and the motion of him starting to bend over at waist, and in the same moment LT spun, gripped the taller man tightly by the throat and smacked his head against the back wall of the elevator. Keith, stunned, was in a partially seated position, his face level with LT's.

"Looks like we're eye-to-eye, now, huh, buddy." LT exuded calm purpose. He took a deep breath. "Allow me to explain to you why things happened the way they did today. I figured Lisa would probably want to handle things like we did just now, you know: 'Yes, your Honor. No, your Honor.' All nice and polite and legal. But there is a different way to handle things—a cowboy way. And if you don't follow the instructions the judge gave you and the ones I'm fixing to give you, I will be pleased to 'go rodeo' and we'll settle things between us that way.

"Now let me tell you how it's going to be from now on. Never again are you going to use any ugly words in talking to or describing your ex-wife. In particular, you will never speak critically about Lisa Newsome again in front of her children. 'Cause you know, if you do, it will get back to me."

Lisa had never seen the expression the Keith was wearing before. She wondered how he was going to react. And for the first time she could remember, she felt a little sorry for him— even though she knew he had it, and more, coming.

"About tonight," LT continued, his hand still firm on Keith's throat, "you need to make absolutely sure those girls are packed up and ready to go when their mother comes to get them. No delays, no hesitation, no distractions, no hostility of any kind. If they aren't ready, I'm sending some friends around to help you learn the importance of promptness. I can assure you, you will not forget the lessons they have to teach you."

For the first time, Keith spoke up. It was a sort of slow, constricted groan from beneath LT's grip. "I'll call the police."

The broad smile broke across the cowboy's face. "You moron. Who do you think I'm sending to see you?"

He let go of Keith abruptly and turned back to the control panel. Keith slid the rest of the way to the floor, sitting with his face to the door. LT pushed in the emergency stop button and the elevator started down again. Only then did Lisa realize the buzzer had been sounding through the entire confrontation. And it was only when LT reached over and took his crutch from her that she realized at some point in his movement he had handed one of them to her. Her racing heart and Keith's stunned, motionless silence belied the supreme calmness of the cowboy.

A bell dinged, a red "1" lit above the control panel and the door rolled open. Two deputies stood outside in the main lobby, flanked by the two attorneys.

"What happened?" asked the older, heavier officer.

"Oh. Stretch back there had a fall," LT said casually. "We stopped to elevator to make sure he was okay. He's all right, I believe."

"Oh, okay," the deputy said. "Say, aren't you LT Tolliver?"

The cowboy smiled as he lumbered out of the elevator. "I am indeed."

"Heard you had surgery on that leg," the younger officer said. "They're saying you're through rodeoing."

He stopped in front of the door. "Not at all. I'm out for the rest of this season, but I'll be back in the spring. And I'm going to ride that bronc who busted me up into the dirt."

"I'd pay to see that."

LT leaned forward conspiratorially. "Hey, fellahs, this is my first time in public since my surgery. Nobody has signed my cast. I'd be honored if you boys would be the first."

"Sure!" the younger officer said.

"Let's go over here where I can sit down. Got a pen?"

Lisa stood, holding the elevator door open, watching the cowboy lead the deputies away. She glanced back at her ex-husband, still sitting on the elevator floor.

"So, I'll be over at five this afternoon to get the girls."

She stepped out and the door rolled shut. A feeling of strength and freedom filled her chest. She did not recall ever having such a feeling of vindication and justice fulfilled. She stood silently for a few seconds to savor the emotion.

LT was waiting for her by the large glass front doors of the courthouse, black signatures adorning his cast and sly smile on his face. He opened the door for her again.

"You didn't put weight on that foot, did you?"

"Of course not."

Neither of them spoke as they crossed to the handicap parking lot and got in the truck. And they did not speak as they

77

drove through the streets of Fort Worth toward Lisa's house.

She had no idea what he was thinking, but her mind kept reliving the courtroom and elevator experiences again and again. The expression on the face of the judge as he gradually became fully aware of Keith's deceit and his sullen treatment of the girls was etched permanently in Lisa's mind. This day in court had completely undone and corrected the injustice of her first custody hearing.

Lisa didn't have to glance over at the cowboy to know he was looking out the window, his face tranquil. He had orchestrated all this. What an amazing, mysterious person he was. How much he had to respect and care for her to hire a lawyer and then to face down the much bigger man in the elevator—and he did it with such masterful control and authority, even with his foot in a cast.

She gripped the steering wheel, staring straight ahead. She raised her behind slightly off the seat. Something felt odd between her legs. The crotch of her panties was soaked. She sucked her lips between her teeth. Never before in her life, she realized, had she ever wanted a man the way she wanted the cowboy at that very second. She wanted him inside her and pressed against her and wrapped around her. Every part of her craved him.

She parked in her driveway behind her dusty little Honda, pulled the key from the ignition and sat staring straight ahead. She could tell he was watching her.

"Would you like to come in?"

". . . Do you think you'll have enough time to get everything set up for your girls?"

"Oh, I'm ready right now."

"Well yeah, if you're for sure ready, then I'd love to come."

It was all she could do not to touch him as they got out of the truck and walked to the house. She wondered if LT noticed how her hands were shaking as she dug in her purse for the door key. Did he have any idea how completely, undeniably aroused she was?

Lisa opened the door, stepped in and waited just inside for him. As soon as he cleared the frame, she pushed it shut, dropped her purse and circled his neck with her arms. She kissed him hard, forcing her tongue into his mouth.

When she pulled back to breathe, she spoke. "Fuck me right now, LT Tolliver." Her hands on his face, she dragged him toward the couch. "Right now. With no delays, no hesitation. No—" She kissed him again. "—how did you say it? No distractions."

Lifting her blouse, cupping her breasts with his hands, he gave a little laugh. "I would like to see anything that could distract me from you right now, *Azulita*."

She found herself lying on the big, four cushion sofa, pulling the cowboy on top of herself, tearing at his zipper and pushing his jeans and underwear together down over his hips. He was busy taking off her shirt and bra and jumped as she gripped his half-erect penis in both hands. She worked it firmly, kneading it, feeling it harden and lengthen and rubbing the glans against the part of her belly that was exposed.

"God, I hope you are ready," he whispered. "You sure got me primed."

Kneeling on the sofa, he lifted her legs onto his shoulders and pulled off her slacks and panties, tossing them onto the floor. Lisa's head was lying back on the cushion and she felt him pause. What was he doing? When she opened her eyes and lifted her face to look at his, he smiled at her.

"Every part of you is beautiful," he said. "I see the petals of your little flower glistening wet. It's so . . . I don't have the words. To know you're this way because you want me . . . . Well that's beautiful too."

Then he moved toward her and she felt the cock slip into her passage and ride forward gently until he was entirely within her. He put his hands beneath her hips and lifted her bottom and rocked out and slowly in, watching her eyes as he penetrated the depth of her again and again.

The cowboy shook his head. "I think you got me a little too

worked up here, sweetie. My rider hears that bell coming and I'm afraid I can't keep him from leaping."

Lisa reached up and pulled him down onto her. They had not taken his shirt off in their haste, but it was open and the hardness of his chest on her enflamed nipples was maddening.

"Cum with me," she whispered. She pushed herself upward against the quickening pulse of his stroke. "Cum . . . now, cowboy."

She could feel the growing anxiety of his thrusts within her and her inner lips, of their own accord, seized his member as if to hold it in place. His cheeks flushed red, while his chin and forehead grew white and he pressed and held himself against her. He had burst, she knew—let loose furiously in her passage. And then she came as well—quivering, with shocks tingling from the inner place where they were joined outward through her limbs and body and her tits. And, as if sensing the explosion and yearning to taste it, his lips descended to one stalky nipple and sucked it within his hot, wet mouth.

After a minute of caressing her with his tongue, he collapsed onto her. His rapid breathing slowly diminished until he sighed and spoke to her.

"You know, in the rodeo, if you can last eight seconds, they ring a bell and declare you a man. . . . I think just now I may have done a little more than eight seconds, but that ride was way shorter than I intended."

Lisa slowly shook her head. "LT, you rock my bones. You make me pop just by the way you look at me. . . . Can we just lie here together like this for a little while, with you still inside me as long as he'll stay?"

He smiled. "Oh, that would be delightful, little blue eyes. There's no place he'd rather be. But I figure I made quite a little deposit there, not to mention you were pretty wet yourself. If we lay here, it's going to leave a spot on the couch."

A giggle escaped her lips, jiggling the two of them and reminding her of the phallus lying within her.

"I have two little girls," she said. "Everything in this house is waterproofed. I can just wipe the stain right off after it dries. . . . On the other hand, I might just leave it there as a souvenir. I'm never going to feel the same way about this sofa."

He studied her face. "If we lay there like this, directly old boney is going to harden up again."

"Ha. You make that sound like a bad thing."

"If you leave me to your devices, I'm not sure you'll get everything ready for your girls to come home."

"Oh, I bet I do. And if you can make me pop one more time, then I'll be satisfied and I won't spend the rest of the day thinking of how I wished you would have fucked me raw."

The cowboy laughed. "You're on. No wait a minute—I'm on. Well, actually I'm in. And it so good." He kissed her. "I have a serious question to ask you."

"How serious?"

"Oh, not all that serious. It's just not about sex. I was wondering what you plan to do with the girls tomorrow."

She shook her head. "I hadn't thought that far ahead. I'm still getting used to the idea of having them with me."

"Well, do you think they'd like to come to my farm and go horseback riding?"

"Oh my god. Of course they would."

"Do they have boots?"

"Ha. These are born and bred Texas girls, Mr. LT Tolliver. Of course they have boots. And cowboy hats."

"Think you can find your way out to the ranch about 10 am?"

"Yeah, I think so."

"Great. We can ride for a while and Constanza will fix lunch for us. . . . Say, sweetheart, do you notice that my dick seems to be getting hard again already?"

Chapter 5

He was leaning on his crutches at the end of the gravel drive as the little Honda pulled up, his face alight with the happiest smile she had yet seen him wear. Her daughters in the back seat were gazing all around and seemed not to notice him. Lisa turned off the car and smiled back at him.

"Let's go, girls. We're here."

"Where are the horses?" Nellie asked.

"Let's go."

They straggled shyly behind Lisa as she stopped ten or twelve feet in front of the cowboy. "Come around here, girls. Be polite. This is Mr. LT Tolliver."

He bowed his head slightly. "Howdy, ladies. Welcome to the Tolliver Ranch." He squinted at the taller girl. "You must be Anita."

"Nita," the child corrected him. "Are you the rodeo guy?"

"Indeed I am. Nita it is. And your sis here is Nellie?"

"You have horses?" the little one asked.

He feigned surprise. "Where'd you hear that?"

"Momma."

"Oh." He scratched his head. "Used to be we had some horses around here. But I can't imagine you girls would care about dumb old horses."

"Oh yes," Nita said.

"Yes we do." There was alarm in the smaller child's voice

Felipe and Constanza walked toward them from the big house. Like LT, their faces seemed to glow.

"Ladies, this is Miss Constanza Garza, who runs the inside of the ranch," LT said. "And this is Mr. Felipe Garza, who is the boss of everything on the outside. Felipe, this is Nita and Nellie, the daughters of Miss Lisa."

Felipe swept off his cowboy hat with an exaggerated sweeping motion. *"Buenos días, chicas encantadoras. Bienvenido."*

The girls stared at each other, their eyes wide.

"They were asking me if we had any horses around here."

"Oh, *si, Gallo.* It happens that I just saddled four riding horses."

The cowboy shook his head. "Oh I don't think these ladies want to go horseback riding."

"Yes we do!"

"I want to! I want to!"

He shrugged. "Okay then. Let's ask Mr. Felipe to show us the way."

Nellie began hopping in place. Her sister took her hand and they fell in behind Felipe as he started toward the barn.

Constanza looped her arm around Lisa's shoulder and leaned her head close. "So beautiful, your *hijas, mi dama.* They favor you completely."

"Thank you, Constanza. What a lovely thing to say. I'm so glad to see you again."

The Latina nodded vigorously. "We hope to see you very often." The women hugged. "I'm making lunch for all of us."

As they approached the barn, Rocket came out of the dark interior and stopped, watching the girls intently.

"A dog!"

"Ssh, Miss Nellie," the cowboy implored. "That's Rocket. He thinks he's a ranch hand."

Anita glanced back at him. "What's a ranch hand?"

"A person who works hard on the ranch." As he watched the dog and the girls size each other up, he said, "I take it you ladies haven't spent much time on a working ranch."

Kneeling beside the dog, fending off his copious licks, the older girl asked, "What's a working ranch?"

"Well it's where everybody works. It's not just for show. I mean we don't just ride horses for fun around here. Take this morning. We have pastures full of cows and horses. We have to ride the fences and make sure there aren't any places where one of our critters can get out. Are you wranglers willing to help with that?"

Nellie beamed a beautiful, innocent smile. "I am."

"What's a wrangler?"

"You ask a lot of questions, sweetie," Lisa said.

"A wrangler is a cowboy —or girl, I reckon—who works especially with livestock like cattle and horses."

"I can ride along the fence."

"Well okay," LT said. "Let's go in the barn and see if any of the saddle horses suit you."

Their eyes adjusted quickly inside the great, open doors of the barn. Lisa saw four animals saddled: two, Rex and Trixie, they had ridden before, plus an alert looking little paint and a massive giant of a rust colored horse.

"Senorita Nellie," Felipe said. "Allow me to help you."

He picked up the little girl and set her on the mountainous horse. Nellie's face beamed with a great smile in the dim light. Lisa was instantly seized great reluctance.

"LT?"

"It's okay. That's the right pony."

"Pony? She looks like a Clydesdale."

"No. She's just a thoroughbred."

"The name of this mare is Cinnamon," Felipe said. "That's because of her color and also because she is so sweet." Hands on hips, he stared at the child. "Go ahead, *chica*. Say hello to the horse. Tell her your name."

"Hello, Cinnamon. My name is Nellie."

"Now she will be your friend and do everything you ask her to do."

LT had leaned his crutches against the side of the smaller horse. "Here you go, big sis. Let me help you up."

Effortlessly he swung Nita into the saddle and handed her the reins that, like Nellie's, were tied together in a loop. The paint, inquisitive, tried to look back at his rider.

"What's my horse's name?"

"Scout. Know why?"

"Why?"

"'Cause he's the smartest and the bravest. He always takes

the lead." He looked at her skeptically. "Are you sure you can take the lead?"

Nita nodded. "Yes. Yes, I can ride first."

"Well all right then," the cowboy shook his head dubiously. "If you're sure. My dog, Rocket, knows the way and he's going with us. If you aren't sure where to go, just follow him."

They rode into the sunlight and through a gate Felipe held open for them. Rocket dashed ahead of them as they made their way from the buildings and down a path leading toward a line of small, gnarly trees. It was, Lisa surmised, a creek bed.

Her eyes on the trail and on the dog, her face full of excitement and sacred duty, Nita rode the lead with Scout. Nellie, never losing her smile, rode behind her sister and Lisa followed, riding side-by-side with LT.

"That is an awfully big horse for a tiny little girl," she said softly. "And are you sure Nita should be leading?"

The cowboy shrugged. "A couple times a month we have groups of physically and developmentally handicapped folks come out to the farm to ride. We have seven or eight horses specially trained to give them rides. We put 'em up on these ponies and send them out through this pasture. The horses know just how to act, no matter what the riders do." He nodded toward Nellie. "I've put 300 pounders up on Cinnamon. Some try to get her to gallop or buck. She never budges one step from where she's supposed to go. Never speeds up. Never leaves the trail."

They rode in silence for half an hour. Nita maintained her solemn, joyous vigil on the lead horse. Sometimes, when Rocket would stray to one side or the other to sniff something, Nita would call out to him and he would jet farther down the trail,

"I've been thinking about yesterday," Lisa said.

"Yeah?"

"Almost everybody in that courthouse seemed to know you."

"Well, I been around a long time, *Azulita*."

85

"Everybody knew you but my ex-husband and the judge."

He chuckled. "Well I feel as if Keith and I know one another pretty good now. As for Thomas Wheeler, he's been knowing me since before he got elevated to the bench. I went to school with a couple of his kids."

"He sure didn't let on that he knew you."

"Couldn't." He shook his head. "That might have shown prejudice. I guarantee, though, when he saw I was with you, it perked up his interest. Not that anything he ruled would've been different, but he knew to take you seriously when he saw I was with you. . . . That and Betty is such a dynamite lawyer. Any judge just naturally knows that ruling against her is an iffy proposition."

"What do you mean?"

"Remember how I told her I didn't know if she could pull her case together as fast as she did? Well the truth of the matter is, if she don't believe in a client, she passes 'em off. When I heard her start in with Judge Wheeler the way she did, I knew Keith's goose was in the oven and pretty much cooked." He gave her a sideways glance. "Speaking of which, I hope he didn't give you any sand about the girls coming home with you."

"None at all. The girls were ready. Their stuff was packed and sitting by the door. Not a word was passed between us." She smiled despite herself. "Now the girls were a little confused and excited. I explained they were coming back to live with me and they seemed real relieved." She began to tear up. "And they slept in my bed last night. We sat up past ten watching TV. Painting our toes. Catching up on what's been happening in our lives. Talking about riding horses."

He shrugged. "Well. Hope this doesn't disappoint them."

"Are you kidding me? They've been sprung from hell and are riding to heaven on horseback."

The broad, familiar smile spread across the cowboy's face.

"There's horses!" Nellie cried, pointing to half a dozen ponies grazing along the fence line 100 yards away.

"Good job, Miss Nellie. Did you count how many there were?"

". . . Five. No, six."

"Okay, then. We might see seven or eight more in this pasture."

"Can we ride them?"

"Well no, sweetie," LT said. "Those aren't riding horses. They're racing horses?"

"Racing horses?"

"Yes, ma'am. They're called quarter horses. They're a little wild and very fast. I'll show you." He looked for the dog, who had paused along the trail and was watching the young herd. "Rocket! Sic!"

Instantly the dog shot toward the ponies, barking madly. They turned as one and bolted, disappearing down the trail toward the barn.

Lisa caught her breath. Turned halfway in their saddles, Nellie and Nita stared after them.

"Turn forward in the saddle, wranglers," the cowboy called. "Hang on."

The girls rode on in silent awe. Eventually a barn and farmhouses appeared before them.

"Is that your place?" Lisa asked.

"Yep. The pasture trail leads you around in a long circle and you end up back where you started."

"Mom, there's the house."

"I know, Nita. We're back where we started."

"Mr. LT," Nellie called, "we didn't find those other horses."

"Well, I guess we'll give Rocket a drink of water and send him back out. It's his job to find the horses and bring 'em in."

Felipe was at the gate again.

"He hasn't been here waiting for us this whole time, has he?"

"Oh hell no. Like I told you, the horses know what to do. And Felipe knows exactly how long it takes them to walk the trail."

"Quieres que me ponga los caballos hasta, Gallo?"

"Si, bueno, por favor."

LT slid off his colt and pulled his crutches from the saddle scarab. They helped the girls down and Felipe led the horses away.

"Well, lady wranglers, you sure turned out to be outstanding riders. I'm very impressed. But we aren't through here on the ranch today. I'm going to give you a choice." The cowboy's voice was serious. "As I told you, this is a working ranch and you are going to have to earn your keep around here. Now these horses live in stalls in the barn and sometimes their stalls need to be shoveled out."

Nita's eyes grew wide.

"You shovel all the dirt out of the barn?" Nellie asked.

"No! Not dirt," Nita whispered. "Poop."

"Eww."

"Well here's the deal," LT said, "with my leg all broken like this, I really can't work a shovel while I'm on crutches. So if you two don't want to shovel horse poop, then your mom is going to have to do the shoveling. I guess the job for you two is to go through that door yonder to the kitchen and help Mrs. Constanza fix lunch."

Lisa shook her head dubiously. "I guess I'm stuck shoveling poop. It's okay. You two go on."

"Please tell Mrs. Constanza we'll be finished with our chores and come in for lunch in about 30 minutes."

They had scarcely started toward the house when Constanza appeared at the kitchen door with a great smile, beckoning them. The girls hurried toward her.

Lisa smile wryly. "Looks like she was expecting them."

He cocked his head. "I think she's making some serious cookies and could use their help."

"This better not ruin their lunch."

"Perish the thought. Anyway, the Garza kids are all older now and Constanza misses little ones like yours." He turned to her. "Ready to shovel some shit?"

"Why not? You're sure dishing it out."

She followed him through the center of the barn past a dozen stalls on either side, to dusty staircase that led up into the rafters of the barn. He started up the narrow wooden steps two at a time. Gripped with alarm, Lisa followed him up.

"I thought you said you were too smart to go upstairs on crutches."

"Actually what I said was, not even I am dumb enough to go down marble stairs on crutches. As you can see, these are wooden stairs and I'm going up." When he got to the top, he turned to watch her climb. "Anyway, it's worth whatever it costs to take your girl to the hay loft for the first time."

Lisa paused as she reflected on his words and only slowly climbed the steps. She stood at the top of the staircase looking around. Bales of green-yellow hay were stacked on either side of the opening to the side walls as well as the back wall of the barn. Immediately before her was a platform created by baled hay the size of a king size bed, covered with a great, thick bedspread. Beside the makeshift bed was a folding table with a long, slender bottle in an ice bucket, two crystal glasses and a sliced loaf of bread that was obviously homemade.

"I was going to have a couple lit candles, too, but this isn't the safest place for that."

She turned her gaze to the cowboy. "I take it this isn't the first time you climbed up those steps today."

As she surveyed the suite he had made for them, hot tears pressed at the corners of her eyes. She took a breath, closed her eyes and spoke.

"LT, what did you mean just now when you said you were bringing 'your girl' to the hay loft for the first time?"

He was sobered by her expression. "Well I sure didn't mean to make you cry. . . . If I was being presumptuous making a bed and bringing you up here and all, *Azulita*, I'm sorry."

"It's not that. . . . What do you mean when you say 'your girl'?"

He was stunned and confused by the question. "If I

offended you, I'm sorry. I just thought . . ."

"Thought what?"

"Well. I thought you were my girl. . . . I was hoping anyway."

The tears began to flow then. She sobbed into her hands, sitting down on the bedspread, trying—unsuccessfully—to stop crying. For his part the cowboy was totally dumfounded and dismayed. When her tears at last slowed, he spoke softly.

"Tell me what I did wrong. Please."

She sighed, a deep cleansing sigh. "First you tell me, Mr. LT Tolliver, what does it mean to be 'your girl'?"

"Well . . . to me it means I don't have anybody else. And I hope you don't have anybody else. It means we do fun things together, with each other and with your girls. I guess it means we get to know one another—to know each other's dreams. It means . . . well I hope ultimately it means you decide if you're stupid enough to hook up permanently with a rodeo cowboy." He gazed at her curiously. "This is a problem for you, I can see."

She wiped her nose on the back of her hand. "Well you sure don't know me very well, Mr. Tolliver. If you did, you would see that I adore you. I love everything about you: the red-neck way you talk; that crazy, mischievous smile; your fearlessness; your generosity and humility; . . . your kisses and your wonderful hard dick; the way you make me feel—inside and out. . . . The truth is, I never thought you'd really want me to be your girl. I am very flattered."

He stared at her. "And?"

"And what?"

"And you'll be my girl?"

"Oh yes." She stood and pulled him to her. "Only on one condition: if you promise me no one will come in this barn and hear us making love."

They kissed—a long, sweet, fulfilling kiss. Her eyes closed, she heard his crutches fall onto the wooden floor and he lowered her gently onto the thick blanket. He lay next to her on his side and she rolled onto her side, facing him. Silently they began to undo his other's shirts. As she undid his last button and pulled his shirttail from his jeans, he pushed her bra up from her breasts and paused, gazing at her with his joyous smile.

"You're faster than me," she said, returning his smile.

He laughed gently. "I've only got half an hour to make you cum six times."

"Actually," she said as he unclasped her jeans and ran his hands along her supple buttocks, "it's never taken you that long before."

He rolled onto his back and slid off his jeans and underwear. "Then let's go for ten. Either that—" He pulled her on top of him. "—or just one really good, earthshaking ride that you never forget for the rest of your life."

"I'll never forget one second of the time we're together." Her eyes linked to his, she slid his member into her vagina and pressed down on him with her body and her inner lips. "And please don't ever forget how we feel at this moment. Together. With one another."

With that, still gazing into his eyes, she began to lift and lower her hips, savoring the delicious sensation of the cock riding back and forth. Long, sweet minutes passed before LT put his hand behind her head and pulled her face to his and kissed her, probing her mouth with his tongue. Much as she wanted this moment to last forever, Lisa felt the irresistible approach of her climax. She moaned and lifted her head, closing her eyes.

"Ah, ah." Her limbs shuddered and she felt herself drooping forward onto him. "Fuck me, cowboy," she whispered. "Don't stop. . . . Fill me up."

LT had continued to move up and into her, but paused and drew a breath. "Do me a favor, *Azulita*," he said softly.

". . . Anything."

He raised her shoulders so he could look in her eyes. He smiled. "Sit on my face. I want to taste you as you cum in my mouth."

91

Slowly she began to smile. Shifting to a sitting position, she put a foot on either side of his head and slid her pussy, warm and flowing, down to his face. He raised his chin and pressed his tongue inside her passage. His lips sucked at her clitoris, pulling it into his mouth as his tongue caressed and manipulated it. Lisa tried to remain still as he touched the already sensitive, aroused flesh.

And then he held her bottom against his chest with one hand as, with the other, he slowly ran his middle finger beneath his chin and deep within her, pressing upward against the confluence of her excitement. From the instant she felt it, she knew a climax was only seconds away.

". . . Cowboy."

"Let it go, *Azulita*."

"I can't help but . . ." The orgasm racked her limbs. She quivered against his face. "Oh. LT. . . . Oh god. I can't help myself. You make me . . . cum again and again."

His head dropped back onto the bedspread. He put his forearm over his eyes. "It's good. I love to feel you cum. I love the way you taste. You do get me a little worked up, though." He met her eyes. "Do you have one more in there for me?"

She scooted back gently, grasping and kneading his cock. Milky cream seeped from the glans as she stroked it and coaxed it to firmness, then spread her legs wide and watched as she guided it between the dripping petals of her flower. Lisa tightened her inner lips on the phallus and rocked toward the prone cowboy again and again. She watched the orgasm approach on his worried countenance, and it aroused her once again as well.

"You cum now, cowboy. You cum now. . . . Oh. Oh."

She ceased her rhythmic motion and concentrated on his suddenly necessary explosive pounding upward. And then it was his turn to quiver and sigh and collapse helpless as they climaxed together. She leaned forward, pressed against him, their faces side by side.

Eventually Lisa raised her head enough to kiss his lips. She sighed.

"We're going to have to wash up before lunch. You're going to have to wash your face."

"Yes. We can't just skip lunch. Constanza won't serve the girls until we show up." He ran his fingers through her hair. "The good news is, there is bathroom down here in the back of the barn."

His face clouded for a moment and then he spoke again. "I want to thank you, *Azulita*, for so many things. I counted up again and figured I left out one operation. I've had eleven over the years. I've been in the hospital probably fifteen or sixteen times. And I want to tell you, you are seriously the best nurse I ever had."

"Oh? How many have you—"

"Just you, silly girl. You're the only one I ever wanted that way. And when we're together, it's like it was meant to be. . . . This was my worst injury ever. I did consider hanging up my gear. Then, the other day when you asked me if I was going to keep riding, I knew beyond a doubt that I was going to get well and rodeo again. So . . . I've want to thank you for getting me back in the saddle, my love."

She wiped the tears from her cheeks quickly. "Well what about all the things I have to thank you for? If it wasn't for you, I wouldn't have my girls—not just for visitation but for always. And you have made me feel so beautiful, so . . . desirable. I don't remember feeling this way for years. So, cowboy, you got me back in the saddle too."

He nodded. "I guess we're a pair then. . . . I told you I didn't want anybody else the way I wanted you. Well there's one other thing I never did. I've been waiting, you see, for the right person to take into my house. I've never made love in the big house. I guess I've always thought I would carry the right girl over the threshold and she would be the one I'd make love to in my bed. . . . Well. It's going to be a few weeks before I can pick you up and carry you, but that day is coming. And that will give you time to decide if you want to be the one."